THE ROAD TO HELL

It seemed to Ben Winwood that all his life he had been second best to his twin brother. Jason Winwood had succeeded where Ben had failed, but when Jason is killed in a mysterious car crash, Ben begins to find that his brother's life was not so enviable after all. Ben becomes involved with Jason's widow, and his associates, and through them is ensnared in a web of crime. Is the powerful influence of Jason reaching his brother from beyond the grave, leading Ben along the same road he himself trod – the road to Hell...?

THE ROAD TO HELL

by

Everatt Jackson

Dales Large Print Books
Long Preston, North Yorkshire,
BD23 4ND, England.

British Library Cataloguing in Publication Data.

Jackson, Everatt
   The road to Hell.

      A catalogue record of this book is
      available from the British Library

      ISBN   978-1-84262-533-0 pbk

First published in Great Britain by
Robert Hale & Company 1975

Published in Large Print 2007 by arrangement with
Everatt Jackson, care of Darley Anderson Literary Agency

Dales Large Print is an imprint of Library Magna Books Ltd.

Printed and bound in Great Britain by
T.J. (International) Ltd., Cornwall, PL28 8RW

Chapter One

Ben Winwood arrived home that Friday evening, the thirteenth of June, with a splitting headache. It had begun suddenly with blinding fierceness just after two-thirty that afternoon. He remembered the time because seconds earlier the announcer on the car radio had given the time:

'For all you clock-watchers, here's a time check. It's now two-thirty and forty seconds pree-cisely!'

Ben remembered hearing that clearly and then moments later it had hit him out of nowhere. A shattering pain behind his eyes and wavy lines in front of them. Hell! He felt sick! He felt the car swerve and he blinked furiously to see the road. Taking his foot from the accelerator and braking – not too sharply – was a fortunate, natural reaction, which he realized afterwards had probably saved his life. Plus the luck that there had been no other traffic on that stretch of road at that particular moment. He had pulled into a layby and sat quietly for ten minutes. The pain had subsided a little into a dull, throbbing ache. Gingerly Ben had started the car again. He'd never had a headache start like that before.

Migraine, he supposed. He'd heard people lament about being a 'martyr to migraine'. Maybe this was what they meant. It was certainly no joke!

Ben had two more calls to make and then he'd go home.

The chatty Joe Speigal kept him talking for an hour and a half and then didn't even give Ben an order. By the time he had walked back to his car, Ben felt he couldn't face another session today, especially not with Gregory Lanaghan – his last call for the day. He'd skip it, Ben decided, and go home now. Driving back to Melchester across the moorland countryside, he made a mental note to be sure to call on Lanaghan first thing on Monday morning.

Jason had made a particular point of asking him to visit Lanaghan that Friday, though why, Ben could not imagine. Only on the Monday, four days earlier, Jason had come with him on his routine call to Lanaghan. Ben wasn't due to call at that shop again for another three to four weeks. However, he'd ring Jason at home later and explain why he hadn't called on Lanaghan. Explain, too, the reason he'd gone home earlier than usual. It shouldn't matter whether he knocked off early or not, but it was like Jason to get to hear that Ben's car had been outside his home at five in the afternoon instead of six. Ben changed gear and winced as he made a hash of it and the sound of grating cogs pierced his aching head. He could never make up his mind, he thought, whether it was an advantage or a distinct disadvantage that the Sales Manager – his boss – was also his twin brother, Jason. At times it seemed that Jason Winwood treated him more harshly than he dealt with all the other sales representatives under his authority. But at other times – when the sales figures for the month were issued with Ben's name always at the bottom of the list – it seemed that Ben only held on to his job because of his relationship to the Sales Manager.

As he opened the front door the sounds of the house met him with even greater force than usual. His son of four, Mark, was in the process of winning the world motor racing championship for pedal cars around the hall, whilst Gabrielle, sixteen months, stood in the middle of the circuit, howling loudly because Teddy lay in Mark's path and was repeatedly run over, the little girl being too frightened of the oncoming car to retrieve the toy.

Ben stood in the doorway swaying slightly and grimacing as the noise battered his head.

'Hello, you're home early. I'm afraid tea isn't ready yet.' Was it ever? Ben thought. His wife, Jean, appeared with a loaded basket of washing and dumped it in the middle of the hall. Mark immediately ran into it and knocked it over, the clothes sprawling all over the floor. Jean casually picked her way through the muddle to the kitchen. Ben followed less expertly and ended up disengaging himself from a sheet which wound itself around his ankles.

He scooped Gabrielle up with one arm and Teddy with the other. In the kitchen he removed the day's newspaper from a chair and sat down, balancing his daughter on his knee. Her jammy fingers clutched at the front of his shirt, leaving a raspberry-coloured smear. He pulled a crumpled, but clean, handkerchief from his top pocket and mopped the tears from her face. He hated to see any of his children cry, especially his golden-haired, cherubic, youngest daughter. She snuggled closer to him and leant against his chest, thumb in mouth, and her wails subsided to an occasional sob.

Jean smiled fondly at the picture. 'You've certainly got a way with the kids, darling.'

Ben felt the little heart beating close to his own. Instinctively his arm tightened about his child.

'What do you want for tea?' Jean asked.

'Just a cuppa'll do, love,' Ben answered. 'I've got the most awful headache.'

'Oh poor love.' Jean put her hand on his forehead as if trying to soothe away the pain. 'I'll get you come Aspirin.'

'It's okay, thanks. I'll take a bath later and if it's not gone by then, I'll take some Aspirin.'

At that moment, Mark resumed his Brands Hatch noises and Ben winced as the sound-waves hit his eardrum.

'Hush, darling,' Jean shouted. 'Daddy's got a headache.'

Ben didn't know which was the worst – the motor race, Gabrielle's wailing or Jean's shouting!

Ben closed the bathroom door and locked it with a sigh of relief. He turned the bathtaps full on and minutes later he was enveloped in the hot, soothing water. He lay there motionless for a long time, his mind a blank, his eyes wandering aimlessly about the small room. He watched the steam rise and curl, misting the mirror, condensing and forming rivulets on the blue, washable, steam-resisting, wet-proof wallpaper – as the ads called it. It was the only room in the house, being the smallest, where they could afford to have such expensive wallpaper.

It was also the only room in the house where he could find peace and privacy. Here he could lock the door on the rest of the noisy, demanding household and allow himself to sink into the luxury of a bath and his daydreams. Much as he loved his children, a headache was not the easiest thing to put up with when they were around.

Some little time later he became aware of a knocking upon the bathroom door. With the big toe of his left foot he turned on the hot water tap and pretended not to hear his wife's voice. But her knocking continued and the volume of her voice increased.

'Ben, Ben, telephone. It's...' The next words were lost to him. Then louder, shrilly, 'Ben, Ben, you *must* come.'

He turned off the tap and called. 'What *is* it, Jean? Can't a man have five minutes' peace?'

'Ben, please open the door. It's Chloe on the 'phone. Something serious.'

Jean sounded agitated and nervous. That was nothing unusual, but for Chloe, Jason's wife, to be ringing him, now that *was* extraordinary!

Ben heaved himself out of the bath and wrapped a towel about his waist. Emerging from the warmth of the bathroom, he shivered, and then bumped into Jean who was raising her hand to knock again.

'Oh! Ben, it's Chloe,' she repeated unnecessarily. Ben grunted and pushed past her. He padded downstairs, Jean following close behind.

'Hello, Chloe?' he said into the mouthpiece.

'Ben, I *had* to ring you. It's Jason. There's been an accident.'

'An accident. What sort of...?'

'A car crash. Ben – Jason's dead!'

Ben stood for a long time with the telephone receiver in his hand, gazing stupidly at the faded blue flowers on the hall wallpaper, counting the number in each row.

'Ben – what is it?' Jean hissed close by. She was watching him anxiously, biting her thumb nail. In the silence Ben heard the click of her teeth as she bit right through the

11

nail. He always tried to help her to stop biting her nails, and the words 'don't bite your nails, dear' rose automatically to his lips.

'You still there, Ben?' Chloe's voice sounded sharply in his ear.

He jumped physically. 'Y-yes. I – you mean – he – he was killed in a – car crash?'

'Yes.'

He watched as Jean's eyes widened in horror. 'Ben, is it Jason?' she whispered urgently. 'What's happened?'

'Ben can you come over?' Chloe was saying coolly. 'The police have been. They want you to identify him.'

'*Me?*' For a moment Ben shrank from such an odious task. Then he realized there was no one else except Chloe and, of course, she could not be expected to... 'Oh – er – I see – yes. I'll be right over, Chloe. I'll see you in about ten minutes, no – twenty,' he added, as he remembered his dripping state of undress.

He replaced the receiver slowly and met Jean's frightened gaze.

'What is it? What *is* it?' Her voice was shrill with tension.

Ben did not answer immediately. For some moments he just stood staring at Jean but not really seeing her. He heard himself say in a voice which sounded to come from a long way off, 'Jason's dead. A car crash. I have to go over to Chloe.'

All at once his headache was back with added violence.

'Oh Ben! Oh dear!' Jean's hands fluttered towards him to embrace him and then, as if unsure of what she should do, of what he wanted her to do or to say, she drew back and just stood staring up at him numbly, her soft brown eyes pools of distress.

Ben turned stiffly and padded back upstairs picking his way mechanically through the crumpled washing which still littered the hall floor. Jean's frightened eyes followed him out of sight, then her gaze dropped to the two wet foot imprints he had left on the hall carpet near the telephone table.

The blaring of a car horn penetrated the wall of pain. Ben blinked. He was staring at a light, a green light. A green traffic light. Behind him other cars joined in the hooting match. He became aware of his hands gripping the steering wheel with an intense fierceness. Flustered for a moment, he fought with the gear lever and stalled the engine. Re-starting he moved off somewhat jerkily. Mentally, Ben shook himself and tried to concentrate. Queer, he thought, he felt as if he had had some sort of blackout. Obviously he had driven this far reasonably, but he could remember nothing from the moment when he had replaced the telephone receiver after Chloe's call until now. Nothing of how he must have dressed, gone out to the car, started it and driven away. He could not recall having seen or spoken to Jean again before leaving the house.

Must be shock, he told himself. After all it was his *twin* brother who had been killed. But now he came to question himself, Ben realized he felt nothing. And he was surprised he felt nothing. He knew he ought to feel grief – but he didn't. Neither did he feel pleasure – which he feared he might, in moments when his jealousy and envy rose to the surface. But to feel nothing, absolutely not a thing was – uncanny, and left him with a sense of guilt for not being *able* to care in some way.

He no longer had even the physical pain of the headache.

That had completely disappeared.

As he drove Ben thought about Jason, and suddenly he felt his brother's presence so strongly that he thought that if he turned his head towards the passenger's seat, Jason

14

would be sitting there. Ben's eyes watched the road ahead but superimposed in his mind's eye were pictures of Jason and himself, like a cinematographic projection of his memories upon the windscreen. But he was a spectator from the circle, not a participant in the action. He was completely set apart. He seemed to be two people – one drove the car quite adequately, the other watched a documentary replay of the lives of Jason and Benjamin Winwood.

Childhood: Jason, the strong, determined boy, and Ben, the shadow, always trying to emulate his brother but always the poor second. Their mother had been unable – even if she had wanted to do so, which Ben doubted – of hiding her pride and joy in Jason. Ben had seemed – or so he had always felt – to mean little or nothing to her. 'That's my boy,' she would say when Jason succeeded in something and she would pat his cheek in a fond caress. Jason would laugh and swing her round by the waist – as he grew older and stronger even sweeping her off the ground. The two of them would be laughing with delight whilst Ben stood by watching forlornly, feeling so much the outsider, the failure.

Jason winning the school sport's cup with

Ben as runner-up: Jason top of the class year after year. At first Ben would come second in the class, but after a time, because he could never manage to beat his twin brother at anything, he gave up trying to compete with Jason. Lethargically, Ben had settled for second best, which gradually, because he ceased to make the effort, became third, fourth and fifth best. Eventually Ben found himself floundering about at the very bottom of the class.

As they grew older Jason became tall and broad and straight-limbed, his dark hair always neat, his clothes immaculate. The pencil-line moustache he grew at nineteen completed the suave man-of-the-world image, whilst Ben – the same build and colouring – stooped slightly as if acknowledging defeat. Ben's clothes hung untidily on him and he walked with a shambling gait. His dark hair flopped over his eyes so that in time he developed the habit of flicking it back with a nervous toss of his head.

And then, of course, there had been Chloe.

His thoughts were halted for he swung the steering wheel and turned in at the wrought-iron gates, the wheels crunching on the sweeping gravel drive, and came to stop in front of the white-painted front door, the huge brass knocker glinting in the evening sunlight.

Not for the first time did Ben marvel at the grandeur of Jason's home compared to his own semi-detached.

Chloe greeted him with apparent calmness when she opened the door.

Ben followed her into the lounge and stood, awkwardly, in the centre of the room. Chloe sat on the huge, deep-cushioned settee and curled her legs up. One of the best three-piece suites their firm manufactured, Ben thought irrationally. He didn't know what to say so he just waited, feeling and looking embarrassed.

Chloe smiled a pathetic, almost helpless little smile. 'Thank you for coming, Ben.'

'It's – that's all right,' Ben said, and sat down quickly in one of the armchairs. Again he waited for her to speak.

'It's so sudden, isn't it?' Chloe said.

Ben nodded.

'The police are sure it's him, but they'd like you to go and identify him.'

Ben jumped physically. 'Me! Is it really necessary? I mean...'

'Apparently, so there can be no mistake, you know. I did tell you on the 'phone.'

'Did you? Oh yes.'

Silence. They both began speaking together.

'What...?'

'I suppose...'

'Sorry...'

'No, you...'

'I was going to say,' Chloe continued calmly, 'I suppose you'd like to know what happened – at least as far as I know it at present.'

Ben nodded.

'Jason had to go south on Wednesday afternoon, and was returning home today. Apparently the car just ran off the road and hit a tree.'

Ben stared at her, mystified.

Chloe shrugged. 'No skid marks, no other vehicle involved. Just a bee-line for a tree.'

Ben shuddered. 'He must have been taken ill or...'

'Perhaps. They'll make some investigations, I suppose. What do they call it – a post mortem? And some tests on the car to see if it was mechanical failure.'

'When did it happen?'

'Just after two-thirty this afternoon.'

Ben's heart seemed to stop momentarily and his hands felt clammy. He'd never

18

believed all that guff about twins feeling the same pain, especially not between himself and Jason.

But his violent headache had begun just after two-thirty that afternoon.

Chloe's voice was coming from a long way off and Ben had to concentrate very hard before he could take in what she was saying.

'...Jason saw to all that sort of thing. I just don't know where to start sorting everything out. You will help me, Ben won't you?' She was standing in front of him now. Suddenly she knelt down and ran her slender fingers up and down the lapels of his jacket, caressingly. From time to time as she spoke, she glanced up at him from under eye-lashes, heavy with mascara, then her glance would drop coyly. 'I'll need your help, Ben. Now. I'm not asking for Jason's sake – but for my own. For what we once meant to each other.' The eyes – provocative blue – gazed into his. 'We were once friends, weren't we, Ben? Good friends.'

Ben swallowed hard and then nodded, not trusting himself to speak.

'So will you help me?' There was appeal in her eyes, a tear trembled on a lower lash.

Again Ben just nodded.

Chloe stood up and again she was the

composed, mature woman in command of herself and the situation. They talked for a while longer about the arrangements which would have to be made and Ben promised to call again the next afternoon.

'I'd better go and – get it over with. The identification. Do you know where I have to go?'

'Byron Road Police Station.'

'Why, that's right the other side of town.'

Chloe nodded. 'Yes. The accident happened some distance away. About twenty miles from town. Evidently Byron Road is the headquarters for that area.'

As Ben stood up to leave, Chloe came and stood close to him, once again the appealing, helpless look in her eyes. 'Ben, I hate to have to ask you,' she said hesitantly, 'but do you think – you – could you lend me some money? It's been so sudden – I mean, Jason...'

'Of course, of course,' Ben said hurriedly, pushing aside thoughts of his own financial straits. He pulled out the only money he had in his wallet – a five-pound note.

Smiling like a cat with the cream, Chloe flicked it adroitly from his fingers. But her voice belied the satisfaction in her eyes as she said apologetically, 'I am sorry to have to ask you, but...'

'Of course,' Ben said again. 'Any time.' Though silently he prayed she would not take him up on that. Just how he was going to manage until the end of the month when he could reclaim his travelling expenses, he didn't know. But if Chloe, poor brave Chloe, needed it, then somehow he would manage.

Ben might not have been so sympathetically inclined towards his sister-in-law had he seen her actions a few moments after he left her house.

Impatiently, she brushed aside the unshed tears and a slow smile curved her lips. She sauntered across the thick-piled carpet to a small regency bureau and opened the lid. From a tiny drawer she pulled a thick wad of five pound notes and, still smiling softly, a gleam of triumph in her eyes, she placed the one Ben had given her beneath the rubber band holding the notes. Idly, she flicked them through her fingers, her mind on hidden thoughts.

They were kind to him at the police station. Ben had always been rather afraid of policemen: the uniform, the epitome of authority. He'd never had anything to do with them – except once. As a thin, shy twelve-year-old he'd found a purse with one pound ten shillings in it. Not a vast sum, but a fortune to an impoverished schoolboy.

'You lucky devil,' Jason had laughed.

'Why, I shan't *keep* it! I shall take it to the police station,' Ben had said, shocked at the suggestion in Jason's words.

'Don't be so daft. Finders – keepers,' Jason had scoffed.

'Oh no,' Ben had cried, wide-eyed. 'That's stealing.'

Jason had roared with laughter. 'Ya' yeller-livered softie.' But he'd not tried to take the purse away from the weaker Ben, which he could easily have done. Instead he shrugged his shoulders and walked off down the street kicking a tin-can in front of him.

With the sound of the rattling tin ringing in his ears, Ben, with an unusual display of stubbornness, of resistance to his brother, had turned towards the police station.

The burly desk sergeant who took down all the particulars of his find, had been solemn, dignified and frightening to the young boy, who felt pangs of guilt because his brother – his twin brother, who was always right – had called him a coward to be handing in the purse.

Now he found the police were helpful, efficient and quietly sympathetic. The identification passed quickly. It was Jason certainly, but his face was bruised down the right-hand side, and his forehead and eyes lacerated badly.

That explained the raging headache, Ben thought, and then shook himself for allowing such superstitious thoughts to run riot.

'Do you feel up to answering some questions for us, Mr Winwood?' Sergeant Porter asked. 'We don't like having to trouble you at such a time, but we have to make enquiries into all the possibilities as to how the accident occurred.'

'Of course, of course,' Ben answered mechanically. He could not blot out the picture of Jason's mutilated face.

'Sit down, sir. Would you like a cup of tea?'

'Please,' Ben nodded, still somewhat dazed. The sergeant gave instructions to a young policeman and then sat down on the opposite side of the desk.

'Cigarette, Mr Winwood? Do you smoke?'

Before he realized just what he was doing his hand was reaching out and extracting one from the proffered packet. 'Thanks – that is – I don't normally, but I think I could do with one right now.'

That was another difference between himself and his twin. Jason had smoked like a chimney, whilst Ben had always hated it.

He coughed a little as the smoke hit his throat, but nevertheless, strangely, he soon felt a little calmer.

'Now, sir,' Sergeant Porter flicked open his notebook, 'do you happen to know why your brother happened to be travelling on that particular stretch of road today and where he might have been?'

'No – no, I don't.' Ben spoke in all honesty. 'Chloe – that's his wife – said he went south on Wednesday and was returning home today.'

'Did she say exactly where he'd been down south?'

'No.'

'Could it have been anything to do with business, with his work?'

'It could have been, I suppose,' Ben said doubtfully, then shrugged his shoulders and flicked back his drooping hair. 'But I'm not up with all the ins and outs of a Sales Manager's duties.'

Ben saw the sergeant's eyebrows rise slightly, and realized he had not been able to keep the bitterness from his voice.

'We both work – worked – for the same

firm. Both started off as Sales Reps sixteen years ago. Jason got promoted over the years. He's been Sales Manager for the past five years.'

A pause, then Ben added as casually as he could. 'I'm still a Sales Rep with the same area I had when we first started.'

The sergeant made no comment but jotted down a few notes – illegible to Ben – on his pad.

After a few more questions – to which Ben knew he was only able to give negative, unhelpful answers, the sergeant said: 'Well, sir, if you do happen to think of anything – or indeed learn of anything – which may throw some light on this accident, I'd be obliged if you'd give this station a ring.'

Ben nodded.

'You'll be required to attend the inquest, Mr Winwood, to give evidence of identification,' Sergeant Porter went on. 'The Coroner has been informed, and he will open the inquest on Monday afternoon at two o'clock.'

'Oh – yes – er – where…?'

'In the court here, sir, attached to the station.'

Driving home, Ben realized he'd better call and see his mother. He glanced at the small clock in the dash-board. Ten to ten already. He shrank from the task and debated with himself whether he could leave it until the morning.

With a sigh of resignation he took the next right-hand turn in the direction of the terraced home of Mrs Clementine Winwood.

When Mrs Winwood senior opened the door to her son, it was impossible to guess whether she knew or not. As always, Ben quailed at the sight of the formidable figure, more impressive still silhouetted against the hall light. She was a tall, spare woman, straight-backed, her carriage proud. Her grey hair was swept high on her head in soft waves – the only 'soft' thing about her. Her features were sharp – a hooked nose, a pointed chin, a small mouth with shrunken, almost non-existent lips. Her eyes were bright, perceptive and ruthless.

She opened the door wider, turned and preceded Ben into the living room. Not a word was spoken until she was sitting in the hard-backed chair near the fireplace. The room was cold for during the summer months no fires were – or ever had been – allowed in this household.

Ben hovered, nervously, near the window.

'You took your time getting here, didn't you?' Speaking in her normal, clipped manner, nothing in his mother's voice gave Ben any indication as to whether she had heard the news. But her words were strange.

'How – how do you mean? Do you – I mean...'

Mrs Winwood gave a click of exasperation. How many times had Ben heard it directed at him? 'Chloe 'phoned the shop on the corner with a message.'

'Oh. Then – then you know?'

'Of course. Though it's as well I didn't have to rely on you.'

Ben sat down on the settee leaning forward, his elbows resting on his knees, his hands clasped in front of him. 'I've been at the police station.'

'Excuses. Always excuses from *you.*'

There was silence between them. Ben did not know what to say and presumably his mother had nothing more to say to him, for she would never be lost for words. He was surprised, even though he knew her to be a hard woman, that she still showed no trace of emotion at the death of 'her boy'. The only times she had ever displayed anything approaching emotion, had been towards Jason. Yet there she sat, stiff-backed, her hands folded neatly in her lap, her gaze fixed on some point on the wall.

'To think,' she said at last, and there was a world of bitterness in her voice, 'that it had to be *Jason*...'

And between them lay the unspoken words 'instead of you'. It was like dealing Ben a vicious blow in the guts and he sat waiting for the hurt to hit him. But it never came. It was as if his mother were referring to someone else. As if her silent accusation were directed at another person and not at Ben himself.

There was nothing else to say, so Ben left.

He would never understand his mother, he thought, as he drove home. For all her apparent hardness, Jason had been her Achilles heel. He was the only person to whom she had ever shown any affection. Yet he had treated her abominably. Promising to come and see her, and then weeks rolled by before he turned up, whilst Ben had gone every Monday evening to see her ever since he had married and left home. And all she could ever do was to talk about Jason, who had treated her callously, almost cruelly, by word and deed, and yet she loved him still. Perhaps, thought Ben wryly, it was *because* Jason had stood up to her, was not intimidated by her, was stronger than she, that she doted on him. The way Jason had treated their mother, spoken to her and called her the 'old buzzard' behind her back, had always shocked Ben and made him feel uncomfortable, as if Jason were breaking one of the Commandments – which indeed he was, Ben thought. Not that that would have bothered Jason.

'I'll dance at your funeral,' he had once said to his mother as a difficult, headstrong teenager when their strong wills had clashed. Ben had looked on, horrified, waiting for her wrath which must surely come now. But Mrs Winwood had merely smiled and patted Jason's cheek. 'Now, now, that's no way for my boy to speak.'

From that day 'I'll dance at your funeral,' had become a favourite saying of Jason's to be used upon anyone and everyone who dared to involve themselves in an argument with him or to cross him in any way. Never had it failed to shock his opponent into silence.

Jason had not lived to dance at his mother's funeral. Instead it would be Jason's funeral they would all be attending within the week.

Chapter Two

As the first stirrings of consciousness roused Ben the following morning, his first thought was, 'Damn, I didn't 'phone Jason and explain why I didn't see Lanaghan yesterday.'

Then, as he became fully awake, he remembered.

There was no Jason to whom he must report. Ben felt a stab of something akin to elation, a sense of freedom. Immediately he felt guilty.

In the afternoon Ben went to see Chloe.

'You don't have to go this afternoon, do you, Ben?' Jean had said. 'It's Saturday. The children want to go to the park as usual. They look forward to it all week. They don't see much of you…'

'Jean, my brother was killed yesterday. Surely you don't expect things to go on just as normal? Not straightaway, do you?'

Jean put her head on one side and watched him. 'I didn't think you were all that grief-stricken,' she said in a matter-of-fact way.

'He was my brother – my twin brother.'

'So you keep saying,' Jean said drily. 'And his wife was – is – Chloe.'

'What's that supposed to mean?'

'Oh nothing,' she turned and left the room. 'Come on, kids. Daddy's too busy to come with us today, but we'll go.'

There was a chorus of disappointed cries. 'Why isn't Daddy coming?' 'He *always* comes.' 'I want him to sail my boat.'

His eldest daughter, Sandra, came and leant against his knee. She was a self-possessed young lady of five, with a manner which was at one and the same time shrewd and yet candidly disarming.

'Has Uncle Jason gone to Heaven, Daddy?'

Her open brown gaze demanded a truthful answer.

'I don't know,' Ben said slowly.

'Do you mean you don't think there *is* a Heaven or you don't think Uncle Jason will go there because he'd been naughty?'

'I don't know,' Ben said again.

'Uncle Jason didn't like us, did he, Daddy? Us children, I mean. He didn't like children.'

Painfully aware that his perceptive daughter – how did they know so much at five years old? – had once again hit the nail on the head, Ben began to contradict her, but Sandra shook her head.

'He didn't. I could tell. You know, I don't think Uncle Jason *will* go to Heaven. Jesus won't have anyone there who doesn't like little children. Miss Brownlow says so.'

Miss Brownlow, Sandra's infant teacher, was someone whose word, often quoted, was law.

'Poor Daddy. You stay at home and rest.' Sandra stood on tiptoe and planted a kiss firmly upon his cheek.

But for once Ben did not appear to be listening to his daughter, nor to notice her tender action.

Jean shooed the children out of the house and there was silence. Ben watched them go. Jean's summer dress was at least seven years old because he remembered her buying it before Julian, now six, had been born. The hemline, which dipped slightly at the back, had doubtless been in and out of fashion several times since then. Once she had been quite pretty, and, he supposed, she still was in a way. But now she had 'let herself go', as the glossy magazines were forever warning their readers not to do. Her curly hair was always an unruly mess, her face devoid of make-up. He turned away from the window as Jean and her brood disappeared round the corner. And, thought Ben discontentedly, the house resembles her. For a moment he surveyed the shambles of the room. Toys everywhere, old newspapers and magazines, unanswered letters and unpaid bills and a thin layer of dust over everything. Suddenly, it irritated him unbearably. Whereas previously he'd ambled in and out of the house, as untidy in his own appearance as was the house, now he could not help making the comparison between his home and Jason's.

In a fit of rebellion on the top of the television – the only clear surface in the room – Ben traced the words 'dust me' in the dust, gave a short laugh of wry amusement and left the house to drive to Chloe's.

There was really no good reason why he should visit Chloe today. As it turned out she didn't even need his help over legal matters that day for everything was still awaiting the inquest. But Chloe's welcome drove all thoughts of the disappointment on the faces of his children from Ben's mind.

The contrast between the house he had recently left and the one he now entered was unbelievable. The deep purple hall carpet – he guessed that took some keeping clean for there was not a speck to be seen on it – was thick and soft. There was a gilt mirror, a small telephone table and a mahogany regency chair with elegant legs, the seat upholstered in blue and white striped silk. Ben had a mental picture of Gabrielle's jammy fingers tracing their way down the delicate material. A glass chandelier tinkled as he closed the front door behind him and followed Chloe into the lounge. She wore a simple, yet chic, black dress, a diamond brooch pinned on her left shoulder. Her blue-black hair was smooth and back-combed high upon the crown of her head, sweeping down in a sleek curve to the nape of her neck. Ben remembered Jean's vain efforts to back-comb her own unruly locks into a pretence of neatness. 'It looks like a mouse's nest,' he had told her once, and she, good-humoured as ever, had shrieked with laughter and hurled a pillow at him.

'It's good of you to come again, Ben,' Chloe said in her soft, husky voice. She sank down into the settee, and, leaning her head back against the cushions, delicately pressed her fingers against her temples. 'I do so *need* someone to *lean* on.'

Ben cleared his throat nervously.

'We used to be such good friends, you and

I, didn't we, Ben? After all, it was you I met first, wasn't it? I used to think you were a *little* fond of me.'

Ben almost laughed aloud. That was an understatement if ever there was one. Fond of her? A little bit? He'd been crazy about her. He'd idolized her and during the few weeks he'd dated her he had thought of no one else.

Then, of course, she had met his brother – Jason. From then on, Ben had ceased to figure in Chloe's life, though he found it hard – impossible – to push her from his thoughts and his life. Not until after she and Jason had actually married did Ben cease to dream and hope that one day she would come back to him. But he might have known – in fact, if he were honest he had always known – that there was not the remotest chance of him beating Jason at anything. The 'courtship' between Jason and Chloe had been short. They had only known each other two months before they came home one Sunday evening after a weekend in London and announced that they had been married in a Registry Office in London the day before. Only then, after their marriage, had he noticed Jean, and, on the rebound, married her. Jean had been there in the background, a typist in the Sales Department of Charlesworths. He'd seen her often enough, spoken to her but all that time no other girl had existed except Chloe. But Jean had been there, quietly waiting.

'You were always the gentle one, Ben,' Chloe was saying in her soft voice. 'Much as I–' Ben noticed her hesitation before she said, 'loved Jason, he – he could be a little hard. Ruthless, at times.'

Ben thought, not so much gentle as defeated by the overpowering personality of his brother.

Still he felt inadequate. What was Chloe trying to say to him? And what did she expect him to reply? Did she want him to make disparaging remarks about Jason too, or to contradict her?

Unable to decide, Ben remained silent. He heard Chloe sigh, then she said. 'They haven't let me know any more yet.'

'Well, – er – everything will have to wait until Monday – you know, the inquest.'

Chloe gave a shudder. 'I don't *have* to attend, do I?'

'Er – no – no, I don't think so.'

'Then I won't.'

'I'll call on Monday evening and let you know what happened.'

'Will you?' A smile of gratitude lit her beautiful face. 'Oh, you are so good, Ben. I don't know what I'd do without you.'

When Ben left her about an hour later, her words were still buzzing about his brain. Chloe needed his help. She needed him. Ben walked straighter, taller than he had done for years.

When Ben reached home again, he found Jean trying to close the front door – unsuccessfully – on a persistent caller, a man pressing some kind of religious leaflet into her hands, telling her it was the true faith, the *only* true faith. As Ben approached, the man turned his beaming smile upon him.

'Ah, good evening, sir. I was just enjoying a conversation with your lady wife. Tell me, sir, do you believe in the Bible?'

Ben saw Jean disappear, thankful to leave him in control. But Ben felt far from 'in control' and his newfound confidence after Chloe's praise deserted him immediately. For ten minutes the man talked whilst Ben made feeble efforts to tell him, politely but firmly, that he and his wife were not interested in him or his leaflets.

'Look,' Ben was able to break in at last. 'Please excuse me. I don't wish to be rude, but I've just had some bad news. My brother was killed yesterday.'

'Oh my dear sir, I am so sorry.' The man was at once full of contrition and, Ben thought, genuine sympathy. 'Is there anything I could do to help?'

'No, no thank you.'

'Then I'll leave you, sir, and please accept my condolences.' The little man raised his hat and trotted off down the path.

Ben closed the front door behind him and leant against it, thankful that the caller had gone. He hated being rude to anyone and always had the greatest difficulty in repulsing unwelcome callers. He received so much uncivility from the managers and owners of stores with whom he dealt in his work as a representative that he shrank from applying the same rough treatment to others. Not like Jason. Ben recalled an occasion years before when a similar sort of religious caller had knocked at their mother's door. Jason had answered it and scarcely had the man opened his mouth but Jason said, 'Not today, thank you.' Unfortunately, the man had complete faith in the need for Jason to hear his words of wisdom. Unwisely he had put his foot in the door.

Jason had looked down at it, momentarily

surprised at the man's audacity. 'I said,' Jason had repeated through clenched teeth. 'Not today, thank you.'

The foot remained.

Jason had drawn the door open a few inches and then slammed it viciously against the man's foot. A moment later the caller was hobbling painfully down the path shaking his fist at Jason and muttering unseemly language for a man of his calling.

Jason had laughed. 'So much for you "turning the other cheek".'

Jean appeared from the kitchen, still biting her thumb nail.

'I'm sorry, darling. I shouldn't have been so cowardly and left you to deal with him. I do so hate being rude to them, and I knew you wouldn't be either. But they do seem to take more notice of a *man*.'

Ben almost laughed. Jason would never have thought that the way Ben had dealt with the unwelcome caller was in any way 'manly'.

Jean waited for Ben to speak, her eyes round and large with anxiety. From the kitchen came the sound of the children squabbling over their tea. Ben went into the sitting room and allowed himself to fall on to the settee. A spring protested with a loud twang. Their three-piece was old and hard and child-beaten. Jean perched on a nearby chair.

'Chloe heard any more?'

Ben shook his head.

'Does she know why he went away or where?'

Ben shrugged. 'Nope.'

'Do you know?'

'No – but then who am I – a mere junior representative – to know the workings of that superior being the Sales Manager? To think that we started out side by side as reps and here I am after sixteen years still with the very same area I started off with. Needless to say, the smallest area of all!'

'Darling, I wish you weren't so bitter about Jason's success,' Jean said.

Ben grunted. 'Well, I suppose it hasn't done him much good now, has it?'

Jean gasped. 'Ben! That's callous. It's not a bit like you.'

How could he explain to Jean his feelings for Jason when he wasn't even sure of them himself?

'Whilst Jason went up the ladder like a rocket to Sales Manager and the Good Life. Another month and he'd have been on the Board of Directors. I know, because he said

Charlesworth had promised him. You should see his place,' and silently he added 'and his wife', as he glanced at Jean – her round, shining face, her hair tousled, her tights laddered and her dress a shapeless rag.

'You have a lot which Jason didn't have,' Jean said softly. 'You have four lively, healthy off-springs, who adore you. Jason hadn't.'

'No,' Ben said slowly, more to himself than to Jean. 'Jason didn't like kids. They irritated him. Sandra was right – though how *she* knew, I dunno. He never *wanted* children.'

Jean snorted impatiently. 'Then that was *his* loss.'

But Ben did not appear to be listening.

At nine forty-five on the Monday morning Ben drew up outside the double-fronted shop of Gregory Lanaghan.

Ben didn't like Lanaghan. He was a small man in stature, but fat. What little hair he had at the sides and back of his head, was slicked down, whilst the pate of his head was a shining dome. His skin was oily, his eyes a cold, watery blue, his hands pudgy and clammy when he shook hands. He greeted everyone with a spirit of bonhomie in a falsely cultured voice.

As Ben walked through the glass door of

the shop, he recalled that on the very last occasion he had been there, the previous Monday, Jason had been with him. Jason had often accompanied him to this particular shop and had seemed on very good terms with Lanaghan – at least until last Monday.

Lanaghan had greeted Jason even more warmly than he ever did Ben, and there was much back-slapping and heads together between them, though Jason had seemed on edge. He'd laughed at Lanaghan's smutty jokes, though a little too loudly as if his humour were forced. He'd talked business with Lanaghan though had insisted on going into a huddle in Lanaghan's office, shutting the door firmly in Ben's face. Ben remembered having felt a little peeved. Wasn't he employed by the same firm? Wasn't it *his* area after all – not Jason's?

Jason had emerged smoking a freshly-lit cigarette. He was no longer making even a pretence at laughter. He had glanced up and down the shop with quick movements. If he hadn't known him better, Ben would have said Jason was nervous of someone.

'Come on,' Jason had said stubbing out his half-smoked cigarette. 'Let's go.' Without a backward glance at Lanaghan Jason had stalked out the shop.

Obediently, Ben had followed.

It wasn't until later that evening that Jason had rung Ben at home to tell him to call again to see Lanaghan on the Friday.

'But didn't you get his order? You were tucked away in that office for long enough.'

'No – no, I forgot to – er – write it down. We got talking,' Jason gave a false laugh. 'You know how it is. Forgot to take a note of it. Be a good chap and call on him again. Don't want Lanaghan upset, you know. One of our best customers.'

Now Ben felt Lanaghan's pudgy hand grasping his own.

'What – no Mr Jason today?'

Ben cleared his throat. 'My brother won't be coming again.'

Before Ben could continue, the smile fell from Lanaghan's face and his eyes darkened with anger. 'What do you mean? Now you tell him from me...'

'Lanaghan,' Ben spoke with unusual firmness. 'He was killed in a car crash on Friday.'

For one uncanny moment, Ben thought Lanaghan was going to pass out. His usually ruddy face turned deathly pale and Ben felt a tremor pass through the man's hand which still grasped his own.

'Dead!' Lanaghan's voice was a hoarse

whisper. 'Oh my God – no!'

'You'd better sit down,' Ben said with more solicitude in his words than he felt.

The fat man was visibly shaken. His face – a sickly white – glistened with beads of sweat. He pulled a white handkerchief from his top pocket and mopped his forehead.

'Oh my crikey,' Lanaghan panted. 'He was only in here last week – with you, wasn't he? And now – oh my *God!*'

'Car accidents are very quick, you know,' Ben said and was surprised at himself for the callousness in his voice.

It was the sort of trite remark which Jason would have made.

'What the hell are we going to do?' Lanaghan mumbled a few moments later, beginning to recover from the initial shock, though he was still shaken.

'What do you mean?' Ben asked.

'Uh?' Lanaghan jumped and glanced about him guiltily as if someone might be overhearing his anxious self-questioning, for he had not been addressing his query to Ben.

'Oh – er – I – well – I mean…' Lanaghan – the smooth, slick Lanaghan was abnormally ruffled. He spread his hands almost as if in despair. 'Well – you know, *you* know.'

Ben thought for a moment, then he shrugged his shoulders. 'No – I *don't* know what you mean. I don't see why the death of the Sales Manager should send the firm into liquidation. There's always someone waiting to step into dead men's shoes.'

Again his own callousness surprised Ben.

Lanaghan looked sick. Then, for a moment, his face brightened. 'Do you mean, *you'll* be taking over from your brother?'

Ben let out a short, humourless laugh. 'Good God, no! I'm the last person on the staff to get promotion of any sort, least of all to the lofty position of Sales Manager.'

Lanaghan's eyes clouded over again. 'God, I'll have to get a smoke.'

He rose unsteadily and shambled towards the pokey little office at the rear of the shop. Emerging, he held out a half-empty packet with a shaking hand, offering one to Ben.

For the second time in four days, without remembering that he did not smoke, Ben took a cigarette. Not until he had half-smoked it did he realize what he was doing.

'How – when did it happen?' Lanaghan asked, taking anxious puffs at his cigarette. 'And – where?'

'About twenty miles outside Melchester. Evidently he'd been south for a couple of

days and was coming back. Friday afternoon...'

'Oh, Christ!' Lanaghan whispered, looking green again. 'And I told him to go...'

Ben looked up quickly. 'You what? What
did you say?'

'I said...' Lanaghan's glazed eyes flickered,
he took a deep breath and then said, 'I didn't
say anything. Er – an *accident,* you said?'

Ben noticed Lanaghan's curious emphasis
on the word 'accident'. Ben watched his face
closely, but Lanaghan had now regained
control of his expression.

'Yes,' said Ben slowly, 'an accident. Could
it be anything else?'

'What?' Momentarily Lanaghan seemed
off-guard again. 'Er – of course not – no.
What I meant was – was it *his* fault or the
other car driver's or...'

'There was no other vehicle involved.'

'*Really?*' Lanaghan seemed surprised and
strangely excited – or was it relieved – by
that information.

'Er – any – er – witnesses to the accident?'

'No – not as far as the police are aware at
present.'

'The police!' Did Ben imagine it or did
Lanaghan really turn a little paler again?

'Of course,' Ben said, 'they're investigating

the accident.'

'Of course, of course,' Lanaghan added hurriedly. 'Er – coming back from down south you say?'

'Yes. Look here, did you know anything about his trip?'

'Me?' Lanaghan forced a laugh. 'Why ever should I know anything about his business?'

Ben could see the man was lying.

He couldn't get anything else out of Lanaghan, but he left the shop with the biggest order for Charlesworth furniture he'd ever taken from Lanaghan – or from any one else for that matter. Was it a conscience salve on Lanaghan's part? Did he know anything about Jason and his trip south? Or was it just that he felt sorry for the bereaved brother?

Ben doubted the latter explanation. Lanaghan wasn't the type to feel sorry for anyone except, perhaps, for himself.

The proceedings at the inquest that Monday afternoon were over very quickly. The Coroner opened the inquest, heard evidence of identification from Ben, evidence of the accident, as far as they knew it at present, from the police, and adjourned the case pending further enquiries. The whole thing was over in less than half-an-hour.

Sergeant Porter met Ben outside the court-room.

'Are you arranging the funeral, sir?'

'Me? Oh – er – I don't know. I'll have to speak to Chloe, my brother's wife – widow, that is. I don't know if she's done anything. I suppose we were waiting to see – well – for this.' He gestured vaguely in the direction of the court-room.

The sergeant nodded. 'I understand. Well, it'll be quite in order for you to get on with your arrangements now. The pathologist will be finishing the post-mortem today and presenting his report. Normally, he would have completed it for the inquest today, but our local pathologist broke his leg last Wednesday and we had to ask another chap to come over from the neighbouring district.'

Ben nodded, hardly listening. He was thinking that he now had a ready-made excuse to visit Chloe again.

Sergeant Porter watched Ben Winwood walk away, then he turned towards the police station. Minutes later he was making a 'phone call.

'Put me through to Superintendent Spencer of C.I.D., will you?' A pause. 'Superintendent Spencer?'

'Yes.'

'Porter here, sir.'

'Mmm?'

'I thought you'd be interested to hear about a recent car accident. One Jason Winwood.'

There was a clatter and an explosive *'What?'* from the other end of the line.

'Yes, sir,' the sergeant continued calmly. 'I only heard this morning that C.I.D. were following some enquiries which might involve this man.'

'Following is the operative word, I'm afraid, sergeant. We seem to be getting nowhere fast. Anyway tell me what you know.'

Sergeant Porter detailed the accident and the events of the inquest. 'His brother – a *Benjamin* Winwood, gave evidence of identification and attended at Court today.'

'Really? Not the wife?'

'No.'

'Mmm.' There was silence whilst the superintendent appeared to be thinking. 'I presume you know the gist of the nature of our enquiries, sergeant?'

'Yes, sir, but just the bare bones so to speak.'

'Do you think this *Benjamin* Winwood has anything to do with the business Jason was in?'

'I wouldn't like to commit myself, sir, but I'd guess *not*. He certainly gave no indication that he knew anything about it. Seemed a bit of a drip, if you want my opinion, sir, not at all the type to be the sort the Big Boys would recruit. Although,' he added as an afterthought, 'Benjamin does work for the same firm – has done since leaving school – just like his brother.'

'*Really?* Hmm. Well, it might be worth keeping an eye on friend Benjamin over the next few weeks and months. See if he changes in any way – you know the sort of thing I mean. I'll get my lads on to it. Thanks for the information, sergeant. Much obliged. Keep in touch if you hear of anything else.'

'Will do.'

That Monday evening, instead of visiting his mother as he had done for the past seven years, Ben was again ringing the bell of Chloe's door.

As he stepped into the hall, he saw Jason's golf bag leaning drunkenly against the telephone table. He remembered how Jason had become obsessed with the game, playing every available moment.

'It's a stupid waste of time,' Ben had told him, 'hitting a ball out of sight and then walking miles to find it just to pop it into a little hole – and then start all over again.'

'It's a great game, boy,' Jason had laughed, flexing his muscles. 'Keeps you fit. I'm a natural at it. First swing out there on the course and the ball flew straight up into the clear blue sky and landed – plonk – right in the middle of the fairway. Do *you* a bit of good to get out there, boy. Get those round shoulders back for you.'

'What happened?' Chloe asked, minutes later as she poured him a whisky and soda and curled herself on the luxurious settee once more.

Ben told her of the events of the inquest. 'The post-mortem hadn't been completed and the car's been taken by the – now what did they call it – the Vehicle Investigation Branch. They take it to a forensic science laboratory and test it.'

'Whatever for?'

'To see if it was mechanical failure which caused the accident. In fact, from what the police said, it looks as if it must have been. There were no skid marks on the road, no other vehicle involved and no eye witnesses. Though a police patrol car arrived about five minutes after the accident – just happened to be on their regular beat. Do they call it "beat" when they're in a patrol car?'

'I don't know. Ben, did they say – I mean, what actually caused his death?'

Ben shrugged. 'I dunno. That wasn't mentioned. They didn't say much actually – the police. I think they're waiting for the various reports.'

'Oh.'

'Chloe, did Jason drink much?'

Chloe shook her head. 'No, he smoked like a chimney, worse than ever just lately, seventy or eighty a day, but he drank comparatively little and never if he was driving.'

'Seventy or eighty!'

Chloe nodded. 'Well, he got through that amount. Used to half-smoke some and then immediately light another. He's been very edgy and irritable just lately. I don't know why.'

'Chloe, we've got to arrange the funeral.'

'Yes, I suppose so. Ben, will you…?'

'Of course, I'll do everything. Don't you worry.'

'Oh Ben, you *are* good.'

As he got up to leave, Chloe came and stood close to him, her perfume strong and enticing.

'Ben, I'm sorry to ask you again, but…' she hesitated and glanced up at him from beneath long, thick lashes, unshed tears shimmering in her eyes, 'could you lend me...?'

'Oh yes – er – of course,' Ben stammered suddenly realizing what she was trying to say. He fumbled for his wallet trying not to remember that it was Jean's housekeeping he was so readily handing out.

Chloe tweaked it from his fingers. 'Thanks,' she said and smiled sweetly. Of Jean's face when she heard, Ben dared not think. She'd be furious.

As the front door closed behind Ben, his recently widowed sister-in-law was picking up the white receiver of the telephone on the polished table in the hall, and, with an immaculately manicured pearl-coloured nail, was dialling a number.

'It's Chloe. Don't count your chickens too early, sweetie, but I think I might have found you a replacement for Jason in the – er – um, *business.*'

There was a pause whilst she listened to comments from the person at the other end of the line.

'Clever boy! How did you guess it was him?' Her eyes, so recently brimming with unshed tears, now shone with laughter and guile. 'I'll have to work on him myself, of course, but you'll have to play your part. Okay, sweetie? 'Bye.'

As she replaced the receiver she held up the five pound note which Ben had given her, then lightly kissed it. Chloe allowed herself a soft, throaty chuckle.

Ben had been right. Jean was angry – well – to a point. She seemed more hurt than annoyed.

'My *housekeeping!* Oh Ben – how could you?'

'She's got no money, Jean.'

'Oh, come *on,* Ben.'

'No – really. I mean, I suppose she will have when Jason's affairs are sorted out, but when something like this happens so suddenly, I expect he must have left her short of cash.'

Jean made some sort of noise that sounded suspiciously like a contemptuous snort. 'Then she'd better think about selling some of her belongings. That mink, for a start, and how about that flat they have in Palma, Majorca?'

'How *can* she?' Ben snapped back. 'Until Jason's things are sorted out?'

'All I want to know is how I'm to feed six

of us with over half my housekeeping gone?'

'Well, you've got – er – tins and that in the cupboard, haven't you?'

Jean cast a despairing glance at the ceiling. 'Then it's beans, spaghetti and omelettes for a week.'

Ben had not seen his mother again, since the day of Jason's death, until the funeral. As the mourners walked from the crematorium, Mrs Winwood caught hold of Ben's arm, her claw-like nails digging into him even through the sleeve of his ill-fitting black suit.

'You haven't been to see me again. You didn't come on Monday, even, as usual.' The words were both accusation and command.

'I didn't think there was much point. You've never wanted to see *me* before. God only knows why I've kept coming all these years.' There was a belligerence in his tone, which surprised him. It seemed as if he were powerless to stop the words which rose to his lips. It was as if someone else were speaking, not the docile Ben. His own surprise was mirrored in his mother's face and he waited for her anger to envelop him. To his amazement, her eyes softened, a small smile quirked the corner of her mouth. She gave a quick nod, a sharp pecking movement.

'Well, come soon,' was all she said.

Ben stopped walking and watched his mother move ahead of him without a backward glance. His initial surprise turned to disbelief. Had his mother really acted in that way, or was he dreaming?

Ben supposed a funeral was a time for the relatives to recall the past life of the deceased, and, in the normal way to grieve over their loss. But Ben could not feel that Jason was dead – his memories of his twin brother were so vivid, he could not believe he would never see the tall, straight figure again, his slow, sardonic smile, the ruthless glint in his calculating smile. Ben frowned as this picture in his mind's eye of Jason faded and was replaced by one which, Ben realized, was how Jason had looked very recently. The smile had not been so much in evidence and often a worried frown had creased his forehead. The brightness of his eyes had been dimmed by some shadow. He had smoked incessantly – about eighty a day Chloe had said. He had seemed on edge, nervous almost, under some sort of pressure. Perhaps it wasn't all roses being a top executive.

Ben shrugged. Daft, he thought it, to smoke yourself to death like that.

That was yet another difference between them, Ben thought, for he did not smoke at all.

Then suddenly he remembered that during the days since Jason had died he, Ben, had already smoked a total of ten cigarettes!

Chapter Three

During the following week, as Ben made his routine calls on the shops and stores in his area, the orders flowed in. His figures for the week reached their highest-ever peak. He couldn't help but feel that once again Jason was responsible. By this time all his clients had heard of Jason's death from the report in the newspaper. Each one greeted him as he entered their shop with words of sympathy, and he departed with a long order for Charlesworth furniture. It was obvious that they felt sorry for him because of his bereavement, and wanted to boost his sales' figures as a form of condolence.

Would he never be able to achieve anything on his own merits? Ben thought bitterly.

A week after Jason's funeral, the Managing Director's secretary rang Ben one morning.

'Mr Petersen would like you to call in at Head Office this morning.' The girl's affected voice commanded him. 'At eleven – sharp.'

At twenty minutes past eleven, Ben was bounding up three flights of stairs, his tie askew, his hair dishevelled, his suit crumpled and baggy.

'Ah, there you are, Winwood,' Petersen said as Ben was ushered in by the brassy-haired, pelmet-skirted secretary. Petersen glanced at his watch, seemed about to remark upon the lateness of Ben's arrival, cleared his throat and then changed his mind.

'Well, now. Sorry about your brother's – er – accident. Terrible, terrible!'

'Thank you, sir,' Ben said for the umpteenth time that week.

'Now – er – what I wanted a word with you about – was – er – well, your brother will be greatly missed. He worked hard, y'know, in his job. We'll have to get a replacement as soon as possible. Sorry if it seems – well – callous, y'know.'

'Not at all,' Ben said with a slight shrug of his shoulders. 'Life has to go on. There's no place for sentiment in business.'

He felt Petersen's eyes upon him. The Managing Director said slowly. 'Funny you should say that. *I've heard your brother say those exact words a hundred times.* Fancy that now! You thinking exactly the same as him. Never realized you were so alike.' Petersen seemed to be musing to himself. 'You don't look alike.'

'We are – were – twins.'

'Really? Ah well, they do say...' But what they did say, Ben never heard, for Petersen suddenly seemed to rouse from his reverie, shuffle his papers and become more business-like. His green eyes flickered over Ben, a penetrating glance. He was a tall, thin man, angular, with smooth grey hair and a thin, pointed face.

'We can't make an appointment until Mr Charlesworth returns from abroad,' Petersen referred to the absent Chairman of the Board of Directors, 'not for an important appointment such as Sales Manager. It leads automatically after five years to a seat on the Board and the title Sales Director. Your brother was due to take his seat next month. So sad, so very sad.'

Ben remained silent.

Petersen cleared his throat again. 'Anyway, I thought you'd like to know the position. The appointment will be considered as soon as Mr Charlesworth returns. He's not due to return for two months, but I've cabled him, and I rather think he may cut his trip short. Winwood's death leaves us in a very awkward spot, y'know.'

'Really? Why?'

'What? Oh – er...' Petersen jumped and seemed somewhat confused momentarily. 'Well – short-staffed – yes, yes, very short-staffed. He sacked his Assistant Manager only three weeks before his death.'

'Yes, I heard.' Ben shuddered inwardly. He couldn't imagine himself in such a position of authority. Hiring and firing people at will with the power to make or break a person's life. No, the responsibility was far too great for a man of Ben's gentle, conscience-stricken nature.

Now Jason, he would have revelled in wielding such power, with no compunction in sacking anyone – whatever the cause.

'You don't know – er – why?' Petersen was eyeing him shrewdly.

'No.'

'No – no, of course not. A matter at Management level.'

Why, thought Ben, did Petersen seem relieved at Ben's denial that he knew nothing of the circumstances surrounding Jason's dismissal of his Assistant manager?

'...of course all the representatives will be in line for promotion – two posts to be filled at once,' Petersen was saying, 'and although I can't make you any promises, you understand, I expect you'll stand a pretty good chance, especially as you're Jason Winwood's brother.'

Ben stood up quickly. Could he *never* escape his brother's shadow? 'I don't want any special favours just because of my relationship to the previous Sales Manager.'

Petersen's eyebrows rose a fraction.

'What I mean is,' Ben hurried on, fearing his words had sounded curt and ungrateful. 'Of course I'd *like* promotion – who wouldn't? But – well – I wouldn't want to let anybody down. It – it must be because I'd be capable of the job.'

There, thought Ben wryly, he'd cooked his own goose now. On *that* basis he'd *never* be promoted.

But Petersen was smiling. 'Of course, of course. Very commendable sentiment, Winwood. But I'm sure Jason Winwood's twin brother must possess the same dynamic business acumen.' He gave a hearty laugh, stood up, held out his hand and pumped Ben's right hand up and down with vigour.

If only you knew! thought Ben as the Managing Director's office door closed behind him.

Chloe said, 'Of course you'll get promotion,

Ben. Why on earth shouldn't you? Here, have another sandwich.'

'Well, I'm not exactly a replica of Jason, am I?' Ben said, taking one of the small, thinly-sliced cucumber sandwiches. Chloe poured creamy coffee into delicate, bone china cups. Handing one to him, she tilted her head on one side as if studying him seriously. 'Oh, I don't know. Perhaps you've not had the same chances as Jason. I think you lack confidence in your own capabilities, Ben.' She paused, then leant closer to him. Ben had plucked up enough courage to sit next to her on the settee this evening. Her long, elegantly manicured fingers gently straightened his tie, and smoothed back the unruly lock of hair which fell into his left eye. Softly, she said, 'I hope you don't mind my saying this, Ben, but if you were to – well – look a little smarter, it would create a better impression.'

Ben, not in the least offended by anything Chloe could say, sighed. 'I know – but smart suits cost money.' Ruefully, he glanced down at the worn edges of his cuffs.

'Why don't you have some of Jason's suits?'

'Oh no, I couldn't!' Ben was startled.

Chloe laughed. 'Oh Ben, you're not squeamish or sentimental surely?'

'Well – no. But it just seems a bit... Oh I don't know.' He looked at Chloe, trying to read something in her face. Was she, in reality, the grief-stricken widow he pictured, putting on a brave face – or not? Only once, that first evening, had he seen tears in her eyes, and that had been only when she asked him for money. Since then she'd shown no sign of distress. Even at the funeral she'd stood calmly, her face a serene mask. How he had admired her self-control. But had it in fact been a mask of indifference? Had she loved his brother or not?

Uncontrollably, desire and hope surged in his heart.

'I see no reason why you shouldn't make use of his suits,' Chloe was saying with practicality. 'You're the same build. I'll get them ready for you next time you come.'

So she wanted him to call again. Ben drove home with a small smile of satisfaction on his lips.

Jean said. 'I don't see how they could promote you. Oh don't get me wrong, darling. I'm sure you'd be fine at the job. But – well – you've always said you had the smallest area and your figures are never top of the list, are they?'

Ben flopped on to the settee, and then winced. He'd forgotten once more how hard this one was in comparison to Chloe's soft cushions. Jean handed him a cup of tea in a thick mug-like cup, and a plate with a rough-hewn cheese sandwich on it.

'You've said yourself one or two of the other reps are just waiting for dead men's shoes,' she said. 'Oh darling, I'm sorry, I didn't mean to say that. I forgot, I mean...' Jean floundered to cover her tactless remark, her cheeks growing pink with embarrassment.

'It's quite true, though,' Ben said, not in the least perturbed. 'They've been queuing up for the Assistant Sales Manager's job ever since Jason sacked him. It'll be worse than ever now. The race for the highest figures every week.'

'Well, I shouldn't join the rat-race, Ben,' Jean said.

'You mean you don't think I'm capable *anyway*.'

'No – I didn't say that. But we're happy as we are, aren't we? Money doesn't buy happiness, Ben.'

A picture of Chloe, beautiful, desirable Chloe, flashed before his eyes. Her carefully made-up face, her neat shining hair, and elegant clothes. Her luxurious home, so befitting her beauty.

Doesn't it? Ben thought, but he said nothing to the happy-go-lucky Jean.

Ben visited his mother the following Monday. As she opened the door, he was surprised to se a small smile on her thin lips.

'Ah Ben, come in.' She held the door open as he stepped into the hall, instead of marching ahead and leaving him to follow her like her lap-dog as she had done for years.

'In here.' She led him into the front room. Still no fire, even though the evening was quite cool. So things hadn't changed that much! Ben thought.

'How are Jean and the children?'

'Oh – er – fine, fine, thanks.'

'And – Chloe? Have you seen her?'

'Yes, yes. She seems to be taking it very well.'

Mrs Winwood sniffed contemptuously. 'She would.'

'What do you mean by that?'

'Oh nothing.'

'Just because she puts on a brave face and hides her emotions, it doesn't mean to say she doesn't feel anything. I think she's being marvellous!' Before he knew what he was saying, Ben rushed on. 'Besides, *you're* a fine on to talk. I don't know anyone who shows their feelings *less* than you do. Or haven't you *got* any feelings?'

Amazement flickered in Mrs Winwood's eyes for a second, then she smiled slowly. 'I've never known you speak to me like that. Well, well, well! It's beginning to show sooner than I anticipated.'

'What do you mean,' Ben frowned.

'Oh nothing,' Mrs Winwood said again, feigning vagueness.

'Yes, you do mean something.'

'Well, since you ask. You've always considered yourself vastly different to your twin brother, haven't you?'

Ben gave a wry, humourless laugh, 'I'd have thought that was obvious to anyone.'

'Outwardly,' Mrs Winwood nodded, 'perhaps. But I pride myself I know you better than most – perhaps better than you know yourself.'

'Just what are you getting at, Mother?'

Mrs Winwood leant forward as if about to reveal the secret of the century. 'You're like Jason in a lot of ways – at least you would be if you hadn't just given up trying to compete with him, and sat back in such a lazy, defeatist's attitude.'

'Whatever do you mean?' Ben was stung to retort. 'Who *made* the difference, I'd like to know? You! *He* was your favourite from as far back as I can remember. What was the point in bashing my head against a brick wall?'

Mrs Winwood clicked her tongue in exasperation. 'That's the only real difference there ever was between you, Ben, if only you could see it. You were never *quite* so pushing as Jason. Not quite so – so ruthless. You always seemed to develop a conscience if anything seemed to get a little out of hand. I suppose,' she seemed to drift off into musings of her own as if not really addressing her thoughts to Ben any longer. 'I suppose Jason had a conscience of sorts, but he kept it well hidden – until things got really hot, and then it was only to get *himself* out of trouble.'

'What do you mean?' Ben said again with irritating repetition. He was surprised to hear his mother talking in this way about her beloved Jason.

'I remember when you were at school. If you were caught up to mischief, you'd always own up at once and take your punishment. Not Jason!'

'Oh, I remember,' Ben cut in. 'You mean

that time he broke the school's only projector?'

'Yes – and he didn't own up.'

'They were days trying to find out who'd done it,' Ben said. 'Then a poor weed of a lad – about three years younger than us – got the blame, because he'd been seen near the Geography Room, where it was kept, about the time it was broken.'

'The headmaster threatened to expel the boy,' Mrs Winwood continued. 'And might well have done so, had not Jason finally owned up.'

'He only owned up because all the other lads gave him the thrashing of his life for letting some other poor little blighter take the blame. Never knew why Jason didn't get the push for it.'

Mrs Winwood sighed. 'And then Mr Burtwhistle gave him another thrashing. He was a good head, though.' There was a pause, whilst Mrs Winwood shot a darting glance at her son. 'But he took some persuading to keep Jason on.'

'You – you mean. He *did* want to expel him?'

Mrs Winwood nodded. 'He said Jason's action in not owning up, in allowing someone else to take the blame, showed a flaw in his character. I argued that expelling him wasn't likely to repair the flaw and that as a head he was shirking his duty in merely ridding himself of trouble instead of trying to cure it.'

'Phew!' Ben whistled. 'I bet Burtie didn't like that.'

Mrs Winwood's eyes glittered with remembered triumph. 'No – I touched his pride and he kept Jason.'

There was a silence between them. Then Ben stood up. 'I must go. If you – er – want anything, give me a ring.'

'What about all the – arrangements?'

For the first time Ben fancied he detected a break in his mother's voice, but her gaze was as clear and steady as ever.

'Oh, I'll be – er – helping Chloe with those. She's not up to it.'

Mrs Winwood gave what sounded suspiciously like a snort of derision. '"Not up to it" indeed! Huh!'

'She's upset – naturally.' Ben found himself defending Chloe with unusual vehemence. 'She can't face all – the – um, well – you know.'

Mrs Winwood's shrewd gaze seemed to bore into Ben.

'Be careful of Chloe, Ben. She's a dangerous woman. Don't get taken in by a beautiful face.'

'Oh really, Mother!' Ben said impatiently, flicking back the hair from his eyes. Despite his implied denial of her insinuation, his mother's words made Ben realize something.

He was already half in love with his brother's widow!

During the next three weeks, again the orders continued to fill the pages of Ben's order book. After the first influx, he had expected things to settle back to normal, but instead his weekly figures rocketed. Lanaghan, in particular, gave him a gigantic list of furniture.

'I – er – was wondering about the Pompadour suite. A Special in cerise moquette – priority order. Know anything about it?' Lanaghan said casually.

'I know the *model*. Don't get much call for it in cerise. You're the only one in my area who's ever had it in that colour. You've always ordered it through Jason before, haven't you?'

Lanaghan nodded. 'But you *know* about it, don't you?'

'Well, I've done the covering paperwork,

of course. Always had to hand it straight to Jason personally for his signature, being a Special Order, he said. Good seller, is it?'

Lanaghan's eyes sparkled. 'Oh yes – it's a good seller all right.'

'No one else ever asks for it. It's not a colour in the pattern swatch, is it? Perhaps we ought to get it included if you think it's popular.'

'No!' The word exploded from Lanaghan's lips like a pistol shot.

Ben looked at him in surprise.

'Look,' Lanaghan said placatingly, placing a pudgy hand on Ben's sleeve. 'Do you really mean to say you don't know what's so special about the Pompadour suite in cerise?'

Ben shook his head. 'No – only that it's an unusual colour. Unusual from our point of view, that is. Probably some people find it quite attractive. As I say, perhaps we ought to…'

'Look,' Lanaghan interrupted. He mopped beads of sweat from his forehead and sighed. 'Your brother got me these – er – Special Orders as a big favour. Maybe, we'd better keep quiet about it for a while. It might make trouble for you. After all, you were involved in it with the covering paperwork, weren't you?'

His words and tone seemed to hold a veiled threat. Surely the obtaining of a particular suite in an unusual colour was not such a crime that it had to be concealed.

'I don't understand...' Ben began.

'We'll leave it a while – just till we see how things work out.' Lanaghan gave Ben a broad wink. He smiled and patted Ben's shoulder again, his confidence returning.

'Have you got a customer waiting for it?'

Again a shadow like fear crossed Lanaghan's eyes and he glanced quickly at Ben and then away again. 'They'll just have to do without it for a while.'

Ben couldn't help thinking Lanaghan made a strange choice of words. He made it sound as if it was a regular supply of these suites to one particular customer. Ben left the shop completely mystified. His conversation with Lanaghan left him feeling on edge, as if there was something he ought to understand – but didn't.

Lanaghan watched Ben go, then swore softly to himself, went into his office and slammed the door. He picked up the 'phone and dialled a number.

'Could I speak to your boss, please.' Forty seconds elapsed, then he said, 'Lanaghan here. Ben Winwood's just left my shop. I've been sounding him out about the Pompadour suite in cerise. A Special. You understand? But he doesn't seem to know much about it.'

There was a pause whilst Lanaghan listened to the voice at the other end of the line.

'Yup. Did she indeed! Well, I reckon she's got a point. *Someone's* got to take Jason Winwood's place and who better than his twin brother. Look, let's leave it for a week or so. Till the Big Man gets back. I reckon I could work on Winwood from my side – same as I did his brother – if you can play it from your angle. You know – promotion.'

Another pause.

'Wouldn't work otherwise. An ordinary rep could never handle it on his own. Never get the paperwork past his superiors. No, he'll have to be Sales Manager.'

Another pause.

Lanaghan laughed. 'Ay, I know, this one's a dead loss. But there would be an advantage in keeping it in the family, so to speak.'

Another pause.

'Well, call it blackmail, if you must. He wouldn't want the character of his dear-departed twin brother besmirched, now would he?' Lanaghan said, his voice heavy with sarcasm.

There was a longer pause as the person at the other end appeared to be enumerating all the difficulties.

'Let's hope it doesn't get to boiling point before we get it settled,' Lanaghan said at last. 'I have to deal with some rough necks on my end of the deal, you know. Oh and by the way, I had the fuzz sniffing round my place a couple of weeks after Winwood's death. Of course they found nothing and haven't been back since, so I reckon it's safe to start operating again as soon as we can. Let's hope the Big Man comes back earlier than planned now this has blown up,' Lanaghan added with feeling, and rang off.

The inquest re-opened four weeks to the day after the accident. Once again Ben attended alone, Chloe shrinking from facing what she called 'such an ordeal', but that evening, she anxiously questioned Ben upon the outcome of the inquest.

'The verdict was "death by accident".'

'I see,' Chloe said slowly. 'So there'll be no further hold-up as regards – well – money?'

'How do you mean?'

'Jason's life insurance. The Company have been withholding payment until they knew

76

the cause of death.'

'Oh I see. Well, it's all a bit strange really.'

'What do you mean?' Chloe's eyes clouded and a small frown creased her forehead.

'The Vehicle Investigation Branch say there's no evidence of mechanical failure in the car.'

'How can they possibly know *that* when it's been mangled up against a tree?'

'They're very clever, these chaps. Same as the Pathologist. He says there was no *medical* reason for the accident. No heart failure, alcohol or drugs – nothing.'

'You mean they can't say *what* caused the accident?'

'No. But there were some odd things about it. About Jason.'

'What on earth do you mean?'

'For one thing there was a bruise on his right cheek, and the Pathologist was adamant that it hadn't been caused by the accident.'

'Oh phooey! How could he tell? I thought you said his face was – well – badly smashed.'

'No – no. Not that much. His face was cut, of course, badly, by the windscreen, mainly the top part of his head. You could still see the bruise on his cheek. I saw it when I identified him.'

'Did you? You never mentioned it.'

Ben shrugged. "Course not. *I* had no reason to think other than that the crash had caused it.'

'Oh well, he must have walked into something. A door, perhaps, whilst he was away.'

'The Pathologist said the bruise had been caused about eight or nine hours *before* the accident. Also his suit. You know how fussy he was about his clothes?'

Chloe nodded.

'The left elbow and both knees were scuffed and dusty and there were marks – sort of rings of bruises – round his wrists too.'

Chloe laughed. 'Sounds as if he'd gotten himself into a fight.'

Ben didn't feel like laughing. 'And he wasn't wearing his safety belt when the accident happened.'

Now it was Chloe's turn to look shocked. *'Wasn't wearing it?'*

Slowly Ben shook his head.

'Aw, come on now, Ben. He never went *two yards* without his safety belt. He was a fanatic about it. He was forever nattering at me because I used to forget to fasten mine.'

'The forensic experts gave evidence that the belt was not being worn, could not have been fastened at the time of the impact.'

'If he had – would it have – saved him?'

There was a silence in the room before Ben said flatly. 'They didn't volunteer that information. I doubt it actually. With a head-on collision like that, but the fact that he wasn't wearing it made doubly sure.'

His words, spoken without forethought, had an ominous, double-edged sound.

'But will all this have any effect on the life insurance?'

Ben looked at her. She seemed more concerned about the money she should be receiving than about what had caused Jason's death. Still, perhaps it was understandable, Ben tried to make excuses for her. Suddenly her bread-winner had been snatched away. It was natural she should be feeling insecure and afraid of a penniless future.

Ben patted her hand comfortingly. 'Don't worry, Chloe dear. I'll see you're all right.'

'Ben,' she breathed and clasped his hand tightly. 'You're such a dear.' She leant closer and her perfume sent shivers down his spine. Ben cleared his throat nervously.

'Perhaps we ought to have a look at Jason's papers, his bank accounts, bills and so on.' Ben scrambled to his feet. 'Shall I help you? How about this bureau? Is this where he kept his...'

Ben was moving across the room towards

the bureau when Chloe cried out, 'No, Ben, no!'

He turned back, startled by the urgency in her voice. For a moment he thought he saw an expression of anger and fear in her eyes, but it was gone in a flash, so that he wondered if he had imagined it.

Now she was smiling and patting the soft cushion beside her. 'Come and sit down and talk to me. I'll sort out all his papers ready for next time you come and we'll have a look at them together.'

The episode had unsettled Ben. There was something strange happening. He felt lost, as if he were being led into something blindly. His feeling of edginess, begun by Lanaghan the day before, increased.

On his way home Ben stopped at a pub and bought his first packet of cigarettes.

Chapter Four

To his amazement, the orders still continued to flow into Ben's order book. Lanaghan was particularly generous with the amount of money he spent on Charlesworth furniture in the weeks following Jason's death. It was really as if he were trying to compensate Ben for his loss. The commission Ben received soared. He was earning more than he had ever done in his life – and he liked the feeling.

Normally, he would have rushed home to Jean to tell her of his success – surprising and unexpected, but for some reason he kept it a secret and he also kept back the extra money for himself, giving Jean only the usual amount of housekeeping. Jean, never one to complain or ask for more – unless driven to do so by rising prices or some unexpected major expense for one of the children, shoes or a winter coat – went blithely on completely unaware of the changes affecting her husband.

Or was she so unaware as Ben liked to think?'

'Ben,' Jean said softly one night as they lay side by side in the same bed and yet far apart.

A grunt was the only reply. She knew he was not asleep.

'Ben, has Jason's death really – affected you?'

There was a silence before he sighed heavily and said, 'Just what do you mean by that?'

'You're different somehow. You seem as if you're walking in a dream sometimes. You don't take any notice of the kids now – and you used to be so *good* with them. Or of me. Ben...' she turned on her side and put her hand on his shoulder, 'you haven't made love to me since before Jason died.'

But there was no response. Ben lay motionless in the darkness staring up at the ceiling. He was thankful Jean could not see his expression for he shut his eyes and grimaced.

How could he make love to his wife when all he could think of was Chloe?

'Ben...?'

'Mmmm.'

There was a long silence before Jean sighed, said flatly, 'Oh nothing,' and rolled back over on to her own side of the bed.

After that Ben could not sleep, and he doubted whether Jean did either, for she continually tossed and turned, though not another word was spoken.

She was right, of course, he had changed since Jason's death. He couldn't seem to help it. He wasn't sure he liked the changes. He didn't want to hurt Jean or the children whom he had always loved dearly, but...

The thought struck Ben with a blinding flash. Why was he telling himself he *had* loved them? Past tense. Didn't he still?

It was a question Ben, frighteningly, could not answer.

Chloe sorted out Jason's papers for Ben to read, as well as several of his suits and shirts.

'You'll look so smart in them, Ben,' Chloe said, smiling. 'It's such a pity to waste them. Why, this dark blue suit, Jason never wore it. Not once.'

'If you're sure, Chloe – thanks. Suits certainly cost a bomb these days.'

Chloe sank down on to the settee and, with an elegant wave of her hand, gestured towards some papers lying on the coffee table. Her blue eyes, big and appealing, gazed up into Ben's. 'Oh Ben, I don't know what I'm going to do. I don't understand all this, but it seems I've no money.'

'What? But – but you must have. Jason earned good money – a fantastic salary compared to mine.'

'I know, but see for yourself. His bank accounts seems to be overdrawn and there are a couple of nasty letters from the Bank Manager.'

Ben sat down beside her and leafed through the papers. As Chloe said, Jason was overdrawn at the bank, and there was a list of figures, which though making not much sense to Ben, could conceivably have been a list of debts.

Ben frowned over this list. The sheet of paper was headed 'L'. Then followed three columns of figures. The left-hand column appeared to be a list of dates from eight months before his death and roughly once every month. The centre column showed varying amounts between one hundred and five hundred pounds. A third column showed a list of amounts which seemed to have the centre column figure subtracted from it each time.

'Look at this, Chloe,' Ben said. 'What do you reckon it is?'

Chloe leant closer to him and Ben tried not to notice her strong perfume, the nearness of her soft cheek.

Ben jabbed a finger at the top figure in the third column. 'Three thousand pounds. Then he takes off that figure in the second column – one hundred and fifty making two thousand eight hundred and fifty and decreasing down to the last figure one thousand two hundred and fifty at the bottom.'

'No, it doesn't,' Chloe pointed at a figure about half way down the third column with a well-shaped nail. 'It goes *up* again there, look, by another thousand.'

'Yes, and then continues to decrease again from the larger figure. Know what it is?'

'No,' Chloe replied.

'It looks to me as if this column,' Ben pointed again to the third column, 'was a debt he owed which decreased as he paid off these amounts.' Ben's finger pointed to the second column.'

'And on these dates,' Chloe added, pointing to the first column. Her fingers rested lightly, caressingly, upon Ben's arm. 'Then before he'd got it all paid off he borrowed a further sum. Ben, do you mean he – I – still owe one thousand two hundred pounds to someone?'

'More probably, if there's interest to be added on.'

Chloe gave a pathetic moan. 'Oh Ben, what am I to do?'

He patted her hand comfortingly. 'Don't worry, Chloe dear. We'll sort it out.'

Chloe turned her hand upwards and clasped his tightly. 'Ben,' she whispered.

Ben's head spun. His breathing became curiously restricted. He leant forward to kiss her, but Chloe moved away so that his lips merely brushed her cheek. Immediately, he was filled with guilt.

'I'm sorry, Chloe. I shouldn't have done that.'

Chloe smiled and patted his cheek, but said nothing.

Seven weeks after Jason's death, Ben found himself summoned to the office of the Chairman of the Company, Mr Lewis Charlesworth, son of Sir Joseph Conrad Charlesworth who had founded the firm of J.C. Charlesworth, Ltd, Furniture Manufacturers.

Nervously, Ben waited outside the Big Man's office. Unusually for him, Ben had arrived twenty minutes early for the appointment. He straightened the already perfectly knotted tie and flicked his hair back out of habit, only to remember that the lock of hair no longer dropped forward over his forehead. A visit to Jason's barber – at Chloe's suggestion – had fixed that.

'A fine head of hair, if I may say so, sir,' had gushed the chatty barber. 'Now, if it wouldn't be out of place, Mr Winwood, may I suggest you adopt the same style as your brother. Ah dear, *what* a sad business – indeed! A fine man, your brother, sir. So elegant in his manner and dress. So business-like. Good job, he had, hadn't he, sir? Yes, a fine man.'

Before Ben could reply, the scissors were already snipping off the soft, unruly brown hair.

'Shorter at the front than you've had it, sir, if I might be so bold. Longer at the back. That'll come in time, sir. I'll shape it now, but it'll have to grow a little before it's right. Now, if I might suggest you use some of this. Mr Jason swore by it, sir, a little preparation of my own.'

'What is it?'

'Well, sir, it'll hold your hair in place without giving it that greasy appearance of some haircreams – *so* out of fashion just now.'

'Really. Well, if you say so.'

The difference the haircut had made, Ben

thought, was quite remarkable. He glanced down at the dark suit he wore – one of Jason's. He ought to be feeling uncomfortable, out of place, looking so smart, but he was surprised to find he did not.

'Would you go in now, Mr Winwood,' the secretary said.

'Ah Winwood, sit down.' Mr Charlesworth sat behind a massive, leather-topped desk, papers spread about him on all sides. Six telephones of different colours were ranged, three on each side. On a trolley at his elbow stood a dictating machine and the intercom to his secretary.

'Sorry about your brother, Winwood. Bad business.' Lewis Charlesworth had a gravelly voice and he spoke in clipped phrases, as if he hadn't time to form a sentence, to think of subject, verb and object. It was the sort of voice you didn't forget in a hurry and one you'd recognize again anywhere. Mr Lewis Charlesworth was not a man to forget. He was not very tall but big-framed. His huge shoulders and arms seemed almost to form a horseshoe shape. He had grey hair and a drooping moustache.

'Thank you, sir,' Ben replied and sat down opposite the Big Man.

'Now, Winwood. Got to fill the gap your

brother left, y'know. Two appointments, in fact. Sales Manager and Assistant. Sacked his assistant three weeks before he – er – a-hem –' Charlesworth coughed, 'died.'

Ben nodded. 'Yes, sir. I did know.'

Sharp grey eyes regarded Ben with a steely glare. 'Know why?'

'No, no, sir.'

Charlesworth grunted and shuffled some papers. 'Well – want to promote from the Sales Reps. Ought to be Jones. Long service. Not as long as you, but good record.'

Ben said nothing. Jones had a good sales record all right. Most weeks he topped the sales lists, until recently when Ben had beaten him into second place.

'Your brother did a good job. Reckon you could. Given chance.' It was a statement not a question. 'Your figures have improved these last few weeks. Going to make you Sales Manager and Jones your Assistant.'

Ben gasped audibly, but Charlesworth hadn't finished. 'Start on Monday. And if you make good, a seat on the Board in five years. Your brother was due to take his about now. Pity. Still,' the Big Man stood up, held out his hand, 'maybe you can take his place.'

Ben rose slowly expecting his knees to give way at any moment with shock. Mechanically he shook Charlesworth's hand.

He was out of the office before he realized he hadn't said a word, hadn't even thanked Mr Charlesworth. He half-turned back towards the closed door, hesitated and then turned away again. It was too late now.

'I don't believe it,' Jean said, and giggled. 'Ben, are you having me on?'

'I wouldn't joke about a thing like that, now would I?'

'But – you've always said yourself you were stuck as a Sales Rep for life.'

'That was before Jason died.'

'You mean – you mean Jason's death has something to do with your promotion?'

'I'm taking his place, aren't I?'

Jean's smile faded. Her eyes travelled from Ben's new, neat haircut, down to his straight tie, his dark suit, smart and well-fitting. A shadow of fear crossed her eyes.

'Yes,' she said slowly. 'Yes, I think perhaps you are.'

Chloe said, 'Ben, that's *wonderful!* I'm so pleased for you. You see, I told you, didn't I? I *said* you had all the potential.'

Ben smiled fondly at her. 'You did.'

The delight she expressed in his success

was like wine to Ben. Chloe had faith in him. Chloe said he could really go places. Chloe needed him.

She sighed and a pathetic smile touched her lips. 'It's good to see something nice happening to someone – to *you* especially, Ben. I need – something to take my mind off things.'

She pressed long, delicate fingers to her temples. 'If only I could get out of this *house* more. It's nearly driving me crazy. I can't even get into town easily now the car's gone.'

Ben was surprised. He couldn't understand any woman being unhappy in such beautiful surroundings as Chloe's luxurious home. And to keep the house as perfect as she did, she must spend a good part of her day on dusting and polishing. Although to look at her you wouldn't think she ever lifted one of her well-manicured fingers in the direction of housework. He thought of his own home – his untidy wife and untidier house.

'If only I could get right away for a while.' Chloe leaned back and closed her eyes.

'Couldn't you? What you need is a holiday.'

Poor Chloe, Ben thought, Jason's death had obviously been too much for her. 'Couldn't you go to the flat in Majorca?'

Chloe gave a long blissful sigh. 'That would be marvellous.' Then she opened her eyes, frowned and spread her hands as if in despair. 'But I can't. I haven't any money. I couldn't raise the fare let alone money to take with me.'

'Won't the insurance money be coming soon?'

'*I* don't know. They take so long these people. Just because he'd only paid one premium they're being *very* careful.'

'Only one?'

'Yes, he took it out about six months ago. February.'

There was a pause whilst Ben tried to do some rapid calculations in his head. 'Look, Chloe, I can't promise anything. But with this promotion, I'll see what I can do to help.'

Chloe sprang up, her eyes sparkling. She looked like a child who'd just been given an unexpected present. She bent and kissed him full on the mouth. 'Ben, you darling! How can I thank you?'

Ben swallowed hard, and though an answer sprang readily to mind, he said nothing.

Mrs Clementine Winwood sniffed and said,

'Must be out of his mind, that Lewis Charlesworth. Of course, I've always said he's not the man his father was. Built that business up from being a small workshop in a back street and look at them now. Factories up and down the country and posh offices for a mountain of paperwork that means very little, I shouldn't wonder.'

'You thought the job top notch when Jason got it,' Ben said with deceptive mildness. 'Maybe they feel I have similar potential to my brother.'

'You have – or had. As I told you not long ago, you just gave up trying years ago. You'll have to pull your socks up now. If you're going to take over Jason's job, then you'll just have to be more like him, Ben.'

Lanaghan, slapping him heartily on the back, said 'My *dear* fellow. I'm delighted. Really. We've always got on well. You deserve recognition after the years of service you've given Charlesworths. Ironic, of course, that you gain through your brother's death. But that's the way it should be. He'd be pleased, keeping it in the family. Oh yes, he'd be right glad you're taking over where he left off. In *every* sense, I take it?'

He gave Ben a sharp nudge with his elbow

93

and winked. Then he laughed and patted his shoulder. 'Ah well, we'll see, we'll see.'

Ben was mystified. What on earth was Lanaghan hinting at? Had he heard of his frequent visits to Chloe's and was putting two and two together to make seven?

'Now, my dear fellow, I take it this'll be the last time you'll be calling on me as a Sales Rep, then?'

Ben hesitated for he hadn't really got used to the idea himself yet. 'I expect so.'

'Your brother still used to come occasionally. Of course, you know that. I hope you will do so too. Like to keep contact, y'know.'

Ben nodded. He wasn't particularly keen on being matey with Lanaghan, but he didn't want to be rude to a good customer, especially considering that it had been Lanaghan's recent generous orders which must have helped Ben towards promotion.

'Look,' Lanaghan's bantering tone faded and his face became serious. 'Don't take offence at this, old chap, but if ever you find yourself a little short of the ready,' he rubbed his thumb and fingers together, indicating he spoke of money, 'you know where to come.'

Ben opened his mouth to protest, but Lanaghan cut in. 'Oh I know you think it won't happen to you – especially now you've landed such a plum job. But you'll be surprised. Your standard of living'll go up. A man in that position must keep up appearances. A new car, a new house even. All on a proper business footing, I mean – a loan repayable over a certain period.'

Ben nodded, but he was not really listening now. All at once the thought of Chloe's face, smiling and happy because he'd promised to help her find the money for a holiday in Majorca. Perhaps this would be a way. Resolutely, he pushed aside thoughts of all the things Jean and the children needed.

As he left Lanaghan's shop, Ben paused to light a cigarette.

His tenth that day.

Chapter Five

At the end of August, the first month in his exalted position of Sales Manager, Ben received his first healthier-looking salary cheque.

It had been a difficult four weeks. He had not realized what an arduous task it was just to sit behind a desk all day long, the recipient of all complaints, of blame for mistakes – other people's as well as his own. He was under fire from those above him to increase sales and from those beneath him if he in turn tried to push them too hard.

It was certainly not the enviable position he had previously believed it to be.

Jones, his new Assistant Manager, was far from co-operative, still smarting, no doubt, from the fact that he had been passed over for the job of Sales Manager. He seemed to be working *against* Ben instead of with him and never lost an opportunity to pounce on any mistake Ben made in an effort to belittle him.

Not that Ben made many mistakes. That

was what was so strange. It was uncanny how easily he had slipped into the routine of the job, picking up the reins as if he had once held them before. Ben had fully expected to be confused and ignorant of his duties as Sales Manager. In fact, he was quite prepared to find himself making a complete bungle of it all. After all, Jean and his mother expected him to do so. To his surprise, he found he had some inner sixth sense as to what he should do and how he should handle each situation.

Perhaps, he thought, it was because of Chloe's faith in his ability.

He cashed the cheque at the bank for the full amount, nearly three hundred pounds, and that evening he gave Jean her housekeeping for the month.

Jean counted it and then looked up, puzzled. 'No extra? I thought you got a whacking great rise this month, with this new job?'

'Yes – well. Lot of tax off it, y'know,' Ben mumbled and turned away. 'And I need to get several things.'

'Can't you even let me have a bit extra, darling? Julian needs new shoes and they are so expensive.'

Reluctantly, Ben handed over another five

pound note. 'I'll let you have a bit more next month.'

'All right, darling. Have you to go back to the office tonight?'

'Yes, I'll have to go back for a while. Mountain of paperwork. Should settle down soon when I get into the job more.'

'Why don't you bring it home with you? I could help you with it. After all, I did use to work in Charlesworths' Sales Office.'

'What?' Ben looked startled. 'No – no – you know how it is – all the files and stuff – couldn't cart it all home.'

'No – no,' Jean's face showed disappointment and a little doubt. 'Of course not.'

'Ben! How lovely. Come in.' Chloe stood framed in the doorway by the light from the hall, a silhouette of perfection.

Ben sank down on to the settee and glanced round the room. Perfect as ever. He was getting to know this room very well, and the more he saw of it the more he liked it. Brocade curtains drawn against the dusk: a soft, shaded lamp lighting the room gently, not the glaring arc-light Jean always insisted on having on. 'Can't see what I'm doing,' she would say, 'if it's half dark,' her lap as always cluttered with the inevitable pile of mending.

But Chloe sat and relaxed against the cushions, ready to pay attention to him. She didn't sit there, like Jean, darning socks, or turning up dress hems, her mouth full of pins. Chloe's lips, full and red, smiled directly at him.

'Look, Chloe, about that holiday.' He fished out his wallet and held out to her the rest of his first month's salary. 'That's all I can manage this month. Would it be enough?'

'How much is it?'

'About two hundred and thirty, I think.'

Chloe wrinkled her nose.

'Isn't it enough?' Ben asked anxiously.

Chloe hesitated. 'It's good of you, Ben. I'm truly grateful. But, you see, there's the air fare – full price. I couldn't get on a package tour or anything so quickly. And then there's expenses when I get there.'

'Yes, yes, I do see.'

Ben leant forward, took a cigarette from a packet, lit it and inhaled deeply. He sat forward, his elbows resting on his knees. A worried frown creased his forehead.

'There's no sign of the insurance yet?'

'What? Oh – er – no.'

'But the inquest's over – the verdict given. What's the hold-up *now*?'

'I don't know, I don't know,' Chloe's voice

broke a little, and her eyes filled with tears. She turned her head away as if to hide them.

'Chloe, darling,' Ben sprang up, crossed the short space from the settee to the armchair where she sat and knelt down in front of her. 'Don't, please don't cry. I can't bear to see you cry.'

Slowly, she turned her face back to look at him. 'I'm sorry. It's just that – I must get away. I – don't think I can stand much more.'

Ben half-turned and stubbed his cigarette out in the ashtray on the coffee table behind him. Still kneeling before her he turned back to face her. 'No – no, of course you can't. Look Chloe. I'll get the money for you somehow. Book a flight as soon as you can. I'll get it, I promise you.'

'Ben – you darling.'

She cupped his face in her hands and kissed him on the mouth. Clumsily, Ben put his arms round her eagerly.

'No, no Ben. Please, don't.'

'Chloe – I love you. You know I do.'

'Ben!' Her eyes were wide, but it was not with surprise or disgust. If anything, there was a look of triumph in her blue eyes, but Ben was too intent upon her to notice.

'I can't help it, Chloe. I suppose I've always loved you. Before you married Jason.

When you used to go out with me. But I lost you to *him*.'

'And now,' Chloe said softly. 'There's no Jason. But there is – Jean.'

Ben's arms dropped from Chloe's waist and he stood up.

'Yes,' he said bitterly, 'there's Jean.'

'And four little Winwoods,' Chloe insisted.

His children's faces floated before his eyes. Julian, rebellious, Sandra, whining, Mark and Gabrielle crying. Was that how he always pictured his children? he thought with surprise. Funny, but for the life of him he couldn't picture them as they surely looked when they laughed and romped and played, or angelic in sleep. Right now they – and Jean – stood between him and Chloe.

'I love you, Chloe,' he whispered again.

'Perhaps it's best I should go away,' Chloe said briskly, and moved over to the bureau. She opened a drawer and pushed in the money Ben had given her.

Ben's shoulders slumped. 'I shall miss you – unbearably.'

Chloe turned round and leant against the bureau, watching him. Her eyes narrowed calculatingly. 'Ben, while I'm away, you'll have to make up your mind.'

'How – what do you mean?'

'I'm not prepared to indulge in a hole-in-the-corner love affair. If you – want me, you'll have to come on *my* terms.'

Ben sat down suddenly as his legs gave. Events were moving too quickly for him, carrying him along on a tide of emotion. Chloe's voice, brisk and emotionless as if she were putting a business proposition to him, whirled about his head.

'There'd be several things I'd want. I need a new car. I can't get to town easily since Jason wrecked the thing.'

She spoke as if the wrecked car were more important to her than the smashed and lifeless body inside it.

'And you'd have to leave Jean completely.'

Ben raised his head slowly to meet her gaze. Her eyes were ice-cold.

'Leave Jean?'

'Yes. Then she'd divorce you eventually, and we could be married.'

With shaking fingers Ben lit another cigarette.

At the beginning of September Ben found that his new status demanded that he attend an executive party held at Mr Charlesworth's palatial home to mark the anniversary of the founding of the firm.

Ben read the gilt-edged invitation card and groaned inwardly. He couldn't imagine Jean amongst such surroundings. Her unruly hair, her frumpish dress – he certainly couldn't remember her even possessing a dress which would be suitable for such a gathering. Her conversation would centre on children – teething, feeding, even potting, he thought with a shudder. No, he certainly couldn't take Jean.

But it would look odd, he would feel odd-man-out if he took no one.

Chloe! Of course. She was the widow of the previous Sales Manager, and his sister-in-law. What could be simpler or more natural? He could make the excuse that their regular baby-sitter had let them down and his wife had felt unable to leave the children with a stranger.

Regular baby-sitter, indeed! He smiled ruefully as he realized how quickly the lies came to mind these days. They never, ever, had a baby-sitter, for he never took Jean out anywhere in the evenings.

When he asked Chloe to go with him, she tilted her head on one side, her blue eyes glinting, a small smile on her lips.

'It'll cost you, Ben.' Her words were teasing, playful and yet there was an undertone of seriousness.

'What do you mean?'

'I need a little more money for my trip to Majorca.'

'Yes, yes. I promised you.'

'All right then, Ben. I'll come and hold your hand at the Big Man's little party.'

She was, of course, a huge success. Ben could sense it as soon as they entered the large room. The men's eyes were drawn towards Chloe with open admiration. The women's gaze rested upon her too but with veiled dislike and envy.

She was dressed, as always, immaculately. A dress in emerald green in some soft, clinging material, which showed of her voluptuous figure to perfection. Her eyes were bright, her hair shining. Ben felt proud that her arm was linked through his.

The party went with a swing. All the members of the executive set from the firm of Charlesworths were there, and a lot of other people whom Ben found out were business contacts and personal friends of Lewis Charlesworth.

There was an elaborate buffet set out in the dining room, and the lounge floor, almost as huge as a small ballroom, was cleared for dancing if anyone wished.

Chloe danced close to Ben, her body swaying rhythmically in time to the soft music. Ben felt his pulses quicken, as her hair brushed his cheek. A photographer moved amongst the couples taking pictures, but Ben, intoxicated by Chloe's nearness, was scarcely aware of the flashbulb pointing in their direction.

Jean threw the paper down on the table under his nose as he spread marmalade on the toast she'd made him, slightly burnt as always.

'And what, may I ask, is the meaning of that?'

Ben took a bite at the toast and mumbled, 'What?'

'That!' Jean's fingers prodded the picture on the front page of the local newspaper. 'There!'

Ben leant forward and squinted at the picture. He saw a couple dancing, close together, the man's arm tightly about the woman's waist. Her hair against his cheek. It was a picture of himself, and obviously, although her face was turned away from the camera, of Chloe.

'Er – well. You see – Charlesworth – er – threw this do at his house night before last

106

and – er – I know you don't like that sort of – er – toff's do, so I – er – went on my own.'

'I didn't get the chance to like it or not, did I? I didn't even know where you were that night.'

Suddenly, as if the anger had drained out of her, and the hurt took its place, Jean sat down heavily opposite him.

'And her, it's Chloe, isn't it?'

'If you must know, yes.' Ben felt his anger rising now. He felt trapped by her accusations, by the reproach in her eyes. 'She was there.'

'No, she wasn't Ben,' Jean said quietly, sadly. 'You didn't meet her there, you took her, didn't you? She wouldn't go on her own.'

Ben rose quickly, the kitchen chair falling backwards with a crash at the suddenness of his movement. 'Hell, why all these questions? Yes, I took her. She's my sister-in-law. She's the widow of the former Sales Manager. What's so wrong that I took her?'

Jean's tear-filled eyes gazed up at him. 'Why didn't you even ask me if I wanted to go?'

Ben didn't answer. He turned away, and as he left the kitchen he heard Jean say softly, in answer to her own question. 'I'm not good enough for you now you've risen so high in the world. I'm only good enough to look after your house and children...'

If she said any more in self-condemnation, Ben did not wait to hear it.

'My dear fellow,' Gregory Lanaghan emerged from the office at the rear of his shop. 'Didn't expect to see you again so soon. How's the new job. Coming along nicely, is it?'

'Not too bad, y'know.'

'Good, good.'

There was an awkward pause.

'Wanted to see me, did you?' Lanaghan asked.

'Yes.'

Another silence.

'Business?'

'No – er – more of a personal matter.'

'Ah – I understand,' Lanaghan said, and Ben had the uncomfortable feeling that Lanaghan understood only too well.

'You said – recently – if I ever needed money...'

'My dear fellow, say no more. I *do* understand. How much?'

'Er – I'm not quite sure. I mean, what sort of sum are you prepared to lend?'

'Anything, my dear fellow. You name it.'

'Er – five hundred,' Ben said hesitantly.

Lanaghan laughed. 'That all? My dear Winwood – I'm owed thousands here and there. Literally thousands.' He case a swift glance at Ben. 'Some of which – due to circumstances beyond my control – I shall never see again.'

Ben reddened and said swiftly. 'You needn't have any fears on that score with me. I'll pay it back as soon as ever I can.'

'My usual arrangement for that sort of amount is to be repayed over six months – one hundred and twenty-five each calendar month payable on the first of every month.'

Ben did some quick mental arithmetic and blanched slightly. 'That's a total of seven hundred and fifty pounds.'

Lanaghan spread his fat hands apologetically. 'I've got to make a bit of profit for lending my money out for six months, haven't I?'

'Yes, yes – of course.'

'Do you want it now – in cash?'

'Er – could you?'

'Of course, my dear chap. Wait here.' Lanaghan disappeared into his office and closed the door behind him. Ben heard a key turn in the lock. Obviously Gregory

Lanaghan did not wish to be disturbed in his counting house.

Ben smoked a cigarette whilst he waited and glanced about him nervously. He hoped no customers would come in and witness Lanaghan handing over a large sum of money to him. Ben felt ashamed of his actions and he was sure Mr Charlesworth would sack him on the spot if he knew Ben was borrowing from a Charlesworth customer.

Chloe needed the money and she should have it.

'Here we are, my dear chap,' Lanaghan breezed. 'All in fivers.' He held out a large buff envelope.

'Thanks very much. I'll pay back in instalments as soon as I can.'

Lanaghan nodded and watched Ben leave the shop. Seconds later he was dialling a number.

'Lanaghan here. We've got him.' Pause. 'Yes. Five hundred. Just now.' Pause. 'No, we'll let it simmer a while. Time to move is when he can't pay it back.' Another pause, then Lanaghan laughed and his eyes glinted dangerously. 'Don't worry about that. I'll make damn sure he *can't* pay it back!'

As Ben left the shop and walked down the arcade between the two shop windows, he bumped into a young man – a hippie. The youth was dressed in dirty, dishevelled clothes, his hair was long and matted. A few tufts of soft hair covered his chin.

'Is he in?' he demanded of Ben.

'Pardon?'

'Lanaghan. Is he in?'

'Oh – er – yes.'

The youth nodded towards the buff envelope Ben carried. 'You been gettin' fixed up, then?'

'Pardon?'

'That all you can say, mate? Forget it,' he added with an impatient snort, and slouched off towards the shop doorway.

Ben stared after him for a few seconds. If Lanaghan was fool enough to lend money to that sort, Ben thought, then he deserved not to get paid back.

'Ben, you're an angel!' Chloe said, and kissed his cheek. Ben attempted to put his arms around her, but artfully, she slipped out of reach. 'A bargain's a bargain, Ben.'

Ben sighed. 'Surely bringing you five hundred quid is worth more than a peck on the cheek.'

'Maybe,' Chloe said slowly. 'But you still belong to Jean. I don't like – sharing a man, Ben.'

He sat down on the settee and lit a cigarette with trembling fingers. Her playing hard to get was driving him mad. If she was doing it on purpose, he thought, to make him want her so badly that he would leave Jean and the children, she was certainly going the right way about it. He couldn't remember ever wanting her so much in his life as he did now.

Instead of his gift of money to her leaving him with a feeling of well-being and contentment, it left him feeling angry, frustrated and dissatisfied.

He drove the car home far too fast and as he entered the house, the sight of the usual cluttered state of the room was too much. Jean sat on the hard settee, her legs up, her feet encased in tatty, dirty bedroom slippers, watching the television.

'Why the hell can't you tidy this dump up a bit?'

Jean's brown eyes looked up at him. The expression in them was like a spaniel who had been whipped without cause. 'It never used to bother you,' she said quietly. 'Why the sudden change?'

Ben spread his arms in a helpless gesture. 'Look at it. Just look at it!'

'*You* try keeping it neat and tidy with four lively kids – *and* very little money.'

Ben ignored her reasoning. 'I've got a position to keep up now.'

'So where's the extra money from this grand position?'

'I told you,' Ben shouted, his anger increasing. 'I had some extra expenses this month. Besides, it doesn't take *money* to keep the house clean and tidy.'

Jean was silent, watchful, hurt and yet even she, usually so calm and patient, was herself stung to anger.

'You should see Chloe's place,' Ben carried on, forgetting all sense of caution. 'After all *she's* been through these last few weeks, the house is still like a new pin – *and so is she!*'

'Ah, now we're getting to it,' Jean swung her feet to the floor and sat up. She squared her shoulders, her eyes were bright and her mouth tight. '*She* has a daily help.'

Ben looked at her in astonishment, then he laughed. 'Don't be daft. She's hard up since Jason died. She couldn't afford to pay anyone – certainly not now, anyway.'

'Oh,' Jean said with deceptive mildness. 'Hard up is she?' Then, as her loving patience snapped. 'So that's where your extra salary went. And I suppose that's where you've been going night after night when you've been supposedly working. And you took her to Mr Charlesworth's do and not me. I haven't forgotten that.'

Ben said nothing and his silence was an admission.

Jean slumped back into a corner of the settee, the bubble of her anger deflated, leaving her small and defenceless. 'So it's true,' she whispered and her eyes filled with tears.

The silence between them lengthened and the sound of laughter from the television only served as a cruel knife twisting in the wound.

At last Jean said, choking on the words, 'What's going to happen? What are you going to do?'

'I don't know,' Ben sighed heavily. 'I really don't know.'

He lit another cigarette, his thirtieth that day.

Chapter Six

Chloe flew off to the sun on Jean's house-keeping and Lanaghan's loan, leaving Ben with no refuge from a tearful wife, a scornful mother, an increasingly demanding job and a grasping creditor.

He'd have to find something to get him out of the house, out of Jean's way and away from the kids.

It was Petersen who gave him the answer.

'Ever play golf, Winwood?' he asked, one Friday evening as they walked towards the executive car park together.

'No – no, I don't – haven't.'

'Fancy a game tomorrow afternoon?'

Ben was surprised to find himself jumping at the chance. 'Yes, I'd like that. But I'll probably make a hash of it.'

Petersen guffawed. 'No need to worry on that score, old boy. Lots of the members – chaps as well as the fillies – miss more than they hit. Old Babbercombe's a prime example. Been a member all the time I've been there and his handicap's about a hundred and eighty!' Petersen laughed again.

Ben smiled dutifully at Petersen's weak joke, then asked, 'Where shall I – er – meet you?'

Petersen gave him detailed directions as to time and place and got into his car – a sleek, low-slung Jaguar.

'You can borrow a set of clubs for a start, till you see how you take to it. I'll get some for you.'

Ben nodded and watched Petersen roar out of the car park.

After Saturday lunch, while he was trying to read the morning paper, Julian climbed on to his knee.

'Are you coming to the park this afternoon, Dad?'

'Mind my paper! How the devil can I read with you crumpling it all up? No, I'm going out.'

'Where?'

'Just – out.'

The boy's lip pouted. 'You used to come every Saturday afternoon. We used to have such fun. I thought you liked sailing boats. Aw, Dad, please come.'

'Yes, why don't you, Ben?'

Ben looked up to see Jean standing in the

doorway. He turned away from her steady gaze, set Julian down on the floor and rose himself.

'I can't. I've to meet Petersen.'

Jean said nothing but gave Ben a cold look. That shook him, coming from her, easy-going, loving Jean, glaring at him with something akin to hatred in her eyes. Then she looked away from him, towards their son, and her expression softened. 'Come on, Julian love. Mummy will try to sail your boat.'

Ben heard Julian's voice protesting as Jean led the boy gently away. 'Aw Mum, but it's not the same as when *Dad* comes.'

Ben paused with his hand on the handle of the front door. What the hell was the matter with him? Once, hearing those words from his son would have filled him with pride. They had been his one and only success – his children. He had loved them and had loved being with them. Now he felt nothing. Only irritation when they cried or were too demanding.

The change in his feelings for his wife he could understand, for now there was Chloe. But he could not understand why he should lose his love for his children. Suddenly he felt a wave of acute sadness as if he had lost something very precious.

He tried to take a step to go after them, to say he would go to the park after all. But he could not move. He sighed, inhaled deeply on his cigarette and left the house.

On the golf course, he lost some of his feeling of guilt and remorse. The breeze was fresh and sharp and white cumulus clouds scurried across a sunlit October sky.

Petersen was waiting for him near the clubhouse.

'Hullo there, Winwood. I've picked up a set of clubs for you from a pal of mine. He's broken his leg, poor devil, so won't be using them for a while. Come on, I'll take you over to the practice greens and give you a bit of a lesson.'

He glanced down at Ben's feet.

'Oh – I forgot to tell you about shoes. Stupid of me. Those won't do, my dear chap.' Petersen frowned momentarily, thinking. 'What size do you take?'

'Eight.'

Petersen's face brightened. 'Ah, that's handy. I take a nine and I've a spare pair in the car. They'll be a bit big, but maybe they'll be okay. Try 'em, anyway.'

A few minutes later Ben was plodding

after Petersen across to the practice greens in golfing shoes a size too big for him.

'Now then, let's show you a spot of putting.'

The next half hour, Petersen spent explaining the rudiments of golf. It was like a foreign language to Ben – tees, fairways, the rough, bunkers, the green and so on. After several putts and a few trial swings, Petersen pronounced him fit to 'have a real go'.

'Nothing like being thrown in at the deep end, me dear chap. Finest way to learn anything I always say.' He glanced at his watch. 'They should be here soon.'

'Who?'

'Oh, didn't I say,' Petersen said airily. 'Mr Charlesworth and one of our customers. We play most weekends. Ah, there they are now.'

Ben turned and watched as Mr Charlesworth and partner approached. Ben felt as if his heart dropped down into the size-too-big golf shoes.

Walking towards him at Mr Charlesworth's side, dragging a set of clubs behind him was – Gregory Lanaghan!

'Hello there, Winwood. Fancy seeing you here. Didn't think you played golf,' Lanaghan greeted him breezily.

'You two know each other?' Petersen

asked with mild surprise, which, Ben had the strange feeling, was not quite genuine.

Ben nodded. 'Yes.'

Mr Charlesworth gave Ben a quick nod of the head, acknowledging his presence.

'Good afternoon, Mr Charlesworth,' Ben said politely, and thought the Big Man seemed friendly enough, though he felt somewhat out of his depth alongside the Chairman of his Company. And distinctly uncomfortable to find Lanaghan – his creditor to the tune of five hundred pounds – one of the party. Ben felt beads of sweat break out on his forehead. If Lanaghan should let slip a word about the loan, Ben's exalted job as Sales Manager would be over before it had scarcely begun.

But Lanaghan was all smiles, slapping him on the back. 'Glad to have you along. Your brother used to come with us a lot, didn't he, Petersen? Got to be a dab-hand at the game by he – er – well...' His words petered out as if in embarrassment, but once again Ben had the uncanny feeling that Lanaghan's discomfort was not genuine.

'Come on,' called Charlesworth's gravelly tones, as he set off towards the first tee, his horse-shoe shoulders swinging. 'Let's not hang about all day.'

As if silently acknowledging Charlesworth's right to command, the other three meekly obeyed and followed him.

The three experienced golfers tee-ed off first, and then it was Ben's turn. He placed the ball, planted his feet roughly either side of it and swung. His club whistled through the air, and the little white ball zoomed up into the blue sky. Ben watched it go in amazement.

'Good *shot*, Winwood. By George, fine shot. Thought you said you didn't play. Reckon you're pulling a fast one on us. Ha-ha-ha!' Charlesworth's shoulders shook.

Lanaghan shaded his eyes, and gazed after the ball. 'I think it's landed plumb in the centre of the fairway.'

'Must be a better coach than I thought,' Petersen murmured.

'Beginner's luck,' Ben mumbled, but he smiled inwardly and began to enjoy himself.

Each shot he played was as good as, if not better than, that first one, and at the end of the nine holes – the number they'd agreed on for an afternoon's game, Ben found his score level with Lanaghan's though five or six shots behind Petersen and Charlesworth. Mr Charlesworth, magnanimous because he had won the game, said, 'Don't get it, me boy. If you've never played before, you must be a natural. All I can say. Remember your brother had the same flair for the game. Damn uncanny, that!'

Ben smiled, pleased with his showing on the golf course, but at the same time mystified by it. He, Ben Winwood, was certainly no 'natural'. He'd always been a duffer at sports.

Now, as Charlesworth said, if it had been *Jason* who had gone out there this afternoon and played like that, then it would have been understandable.

Whatever Jason had touched, he had made a success of it.

But not Ben!

The weeks and months slid by. Christmas came and went. Ben found the pressures of his new existence increasing. Life at home, with Jean, was strained now that she knew the truth about himself and Chloe. And though she said very little to him, her silence was a reproach in itself. He knew he had hurt her deeply, and yet he felt powerless to prevent it as if something was driving him on even against his own code of moral behaviour.

At the office, Jones became openly hostile but Ben could find no legitimate excuse to rid himself of his new assistant for the man was extremely conscientious in his work and meticulous to a point where Ben began to wonder if he was being extra careful so that he gave Ben no possible opportunity to fault him.

Petersen, and from a loftier level, Charlesworth were friendly, though Ben had the uncomfortable feeling they were watching him, waiting for him to make a false move. He continued to play golf with them frequently. Sometimes Lanaghan joined them, sometimes not.

'Have to come down south sometime, Winwood. Got my own private golf course on the Norfolk coast.'

'Thank you, sir, I'd like that.'

'Ha-umph,' Charlesworth grunted and nodded.

Ben felt easier when Lanaghan was not one of the golfing party, for it was embarrassing to be socializing with a man to whom one owed money. The repayments, Ben found, were increasingly difficult to find. He had thought it would be easy, from his new and what had at first seemed generous salary cheque. But there seemed to be so many calls upon his money. Jean demanded more housekeeping – considerably more, and because of how he was treating her in the matter of Chloe, Ben found it impossible to refuse her the extra money. Then Chloe, too, even though she was many miles away, was still a drain upon his pocket. He had promised to collect any mail from her home and in so doing found a number of unpaid bills and threatening letters kept arriving. Rather than have any trouble, Ben paid her accounts for new clothes and several household bills.

Ben usually called in to see Lanaghan on the first of the month – the day after he received his salary cheque to pay off some of his debt. But one month the amounts he already owed were more than his cheque and there was still the one hundred and twenty-five to find for Lanaghan.

'Look, could you waive it this month?' Ben asked. 'I'll make it double next time.'

'Mr Winwood,' Lanaghan said, a sickly smile on his face. 'I lend money as a business, not as a charitable institution. If I let you off one month, then you can't find it next month. I know, it's happened before.'

Ben lit a cigarette with trembling fingers.

'I tell you what,' Lanaghan put a hand on Ben's shoulder in a confidential manner. 'I like you Winwood. I could put you in the way of making a little extra on the side. Think about it. Now, you come back here on Friday night and we'll have a chat. If you get the money before then, well, we'll forget it, but if not…'

It was a curious cross between offering a helping hand and issuing a veiled threat at one and the same time.

Ben left the shop feeling caught in an ever-tightening web. He didn't like it. He didn't like Lanaghan, and wished he'd never got involved with him. Then he thought of Chloe and groaned inwardly. He still wanted her like hell! But would he ever get her? He still had to leave Jean to make Chloe surrender.

Of course by Friday he hadn't got the money. In fact, he needed more than ever. A letter had arrived at Chloe's house from the Electricity Board threatening to cut off the supply unless an account, which had been outstanding for several months, was not paid within the next fourteen days. Chloe was due back soon. He couldn't let her come home to a cold, dark house.

At a little after seven on the Friday evening, Ben drew up outside Lanaghan's shop. He walked into the alcove and stumbled against something soft on the ground.

'Hey, watch it, man. Look where you're

puttin' yer plates of meat.' A voice from somewhere at his feet spoke in Cockney tones.

Ben peered down in the darkness. Sprawled on the floor, half-way across the alcove and leaning against the window was a hippie. Ben heard a shuffling and saw that ranged down the entrance to the shop were about a dozen or so young people – all hippie-types, boys and girls too he presumed, though in the half-light and from their mode of dress it was difficult to tell which was which.

'Sorry,' Ben said and picked his way carefully over the sprawling legs. When he reached the doorway, a tall, rangy youth uncurled himself from the floor and stood up to bar Ben's way.

'Wait a bit, man. W'ot you doin' here?'

'I've – er – come to Mr Lanaghan,' Ben gestured with his hand. 'The owner of this shop.'

'Oh yer. We know who Mister Lanaghan is, don't we, fellas?'

Various forms of assent came from the floor, from a 'yer, we sure do' to a high pitched, somewhat hysterical laugh.

'Look, if yer here about w'ot I fink yer 'ere about, yer'll 'ave to wait yer turn like the rest of us.'

'Wait my turn? I don't understand. What do you mean, wait my turn? Are *you* waiting to see Lanaghan?'

Again the hysterical laughter rose from behind him. Ben felt the hairs on the back of his neck begin to prickle. Who were these people and what were they doing here?

'Are we waiting to see him? You bet yer sweet life we are, an' if he don't 'urry it up a bit, there's goin' to be trouble.'

At that moment the shop door opened and Lanaghan's round face appeared. He seemed about to speak to the long-haired youth and then, seeing Ben, said, 'Ah Winwood. Come in. Quickly.'

'Now look 'ere, Lanaghan,' the hippie's foot was wedged in the door before you say 'knife'. 'No queue jumping. We've been waiting half-an-hour now, and you've let us down the last five months.'

'All right, all right, boy. He,' Lanaghan nodded towards Ben, 'is not here for – that.'

Slowly the youth withdrew his foot. 'Okay then, but make it snappy, will yer? If the fuzz…'

'Yes, yes,' Lanaghan said hurriedly and pulled Ben into the shop and shut the door. 'Sorry about that, my dear chap.'

'Who are they? What are they doing here?'

'All in good time, my dear fellow, all in good time. Now, first things first. Have you got the money?'

'Look, I can't raise it this month. But it'll be all right next month, I promise you. It's just...'

Lanaghan was shaking his head slowly. 'It won't do, Winwood, it really won't.' Then he smiled and patted Ben on the shoulder. 'But don't worry about it. We can help each other. You can help me, and I can put you in the way of a little extra money. You do something for me and I'll pay you by wiping off some of your debt.'

'What – are you talking about?'

'Come upstairs and I'll show you.' Lanaghan preceded Ben up the stairs, past the first floor, then the second and finally up a narrow, rickety staircase to the dusty attic above the shop.

As Ben stepped up into an attic room which was a cross between a storage and a dumping ground for rubbish, Lanaghan switched on a light hanging, together with numerous cobwebs, from a rafter. In the centre of the room stood a three-piece suite – a Pompadour model in cerise moquette. One of the Special Orders of which Lanaghan had spoken.

Mystified Ben watched whilst Lanaghan went to the back of the settee and squatted down on his haunches. He beckoned Ben over. Puffing a little with exertion, Lanaghan slashed the material at the back of the settee with a pen-knife. Ben winced at such wanton destruction but said nothing.

Lanaghan thrust his pudgy hand into the stuffing and groped around. Eventually he pulled out a package. He cut the string and wrapping paper. Inside were several small white envelopes. He took one of these and slit the top, then he took out a small twist of silver foil and unfolded it. Holding it in the palm of his hand, Lanaghan held it out for Ben to see. 'Know what it is?'

Ben peered at it. All he could see was a small amount of white powder in the silver foil . 'No. What is it?'

'Heroin.'

'My *God!*' Ben stepped back as if Lanaghan had hit him. He stared at the man kneeling in front of him. Ben was shocked beyond belief. What the hell *was* this?

'Those – those,' Ben pointed vaguely in the direction of the front of the shop with a trembling finger, 'hippies? *That's* what they're waiting for?'

Lanaghan nodded, still smiling as if he

were enjoying the shock he had given Ben. 'Yes. We've got a nice little business going here. I stay late at the shop, ostensibly "doing the books" and my – er – customers come in one by one for the stuff. They're pushers of course.' Lanaghan twisted up the foil again enclosing the drug. 'The pusher will probably demand about five quid for that bit.'

Ben gasped audibly. Lanaghan, enjoying the melodrama all his own making and Ben's scandalized expression, nodded towards the ravaged settee. 'We get two hundred an ounce from the pushers – that's one hundred and twenty of these packets.' He waved the twist of silver foil at Ben.

'What? You mean *one ounce* is divided into one hundred and twenty?'

'That's right. You catch on quickly, boy,' Lanaghan grinned, his bald pate glistening in the naked light from the single bulb above his head. 'To a junkie that's enough for a fix.'

'And those – kids out there,' Ben asked, 'are they junkies?'

'Most of 'em, yes. They push the stuff to make money to keep themselves supplied.'

'But who do they sell it to?'

'Don't ask me. That isn't *my* business.'

'Do *you* – take it?' Ben blurted out.

Lanaghan looked offended. 'Good gracious me, no! I'm a business man, Winwood. The very idea.'

Lanaghan bent down again and once more groped about in the opening he had made in the settee. He extracted a handful of packets each containing more little white envelopes. To think that such innocent-looking envelopes could hold such evil, Ben thought with horror.

'How – how much is in there?' Ben demanded.

'Should be about forty ounces tucked away in this little beauty.'

'Forty ounces!' Ben did some rapid mental calculations. 'That's eight thousand quid's worth.'

'My word, we *are* quick,' Lanaghan said, with sarcasm. 'You're quite right, old chap, worth wrecking a suite for, isn't it. Mind you, we're not so wasteful. We send these back for repair and refill to – er – well, perhaps I'd better say no more just now.'

Ben pointed with a trembling finger. 'You mean to tell me that all this time *that's* what these Special Orders for Pompadour suites in cerise have been about? *Drug carrying?*'

'My dear chap, your perspicacity truly

amazes me!'

'And *I've* been issuing all the paperwork?'

'On your brother's instructions, my dear fellow. On the *Sales Manager's* instructions.'

Suddenly Ben realized what Lanaghan was up to. He took a step backwards and held out his arm, the palm of his hand flat outwards towards Lanaghan as if trying to ward off the evil influence. 'I don't want any part of it. I don't want to get involved.'

He turned and made for the stairs.

'Wait!' The order was like a pistol shot. Ben stopped and slowly turned to look at Lanaghan. The round, fat face was no longer smiling. The eyes were cold and cruel, the mouth a thin, hard line.

'You are,' Lanaghan said slowly and deliberately, 'already involved.'

'I'm not, I...'

'You're in debt to me. And your brother was in it.'

Ben felt as if his knees were going to give way. He grasped hold of a nearby chair for support. 'Jason?' His voice came in a strangulated whisper. 'Jason was involved – with you – with *drugs?*'

Lanaghan nodded and a gleam of triumph lit his eyes. 'He got into debt in just the same way as you.'

'With – you?'

'Yes. Only more so – over a longer period of time. He kept on and on borrowing more to keep afloat until he had no option but to join us. And neither, my dear chap, have you.'

'I'll pay you back, Lanaghan,' Ben said between clenched teeth, his shock and fear giving place to anger now. 'I'll get the money somehow.'

Lanaghan was smiling again now, with confidence. 'I don't think you will. It took longer to get Jason involved. But I had to get to work quicker on you. We hadn't time to wait.'

'We? Who's we?'

Lanaghan shook his head. 'Oh no. I'm not giving that away. Not just yet, anyway.'

Ben sat down on the top step of the rickety stairs. 'Are you telling me that it was all planned. To get Jason involved in the first place and then, after he died, me?'

'Just so.'

'But what…?'

'What do you have to do?' Lanaghan said. 'I wasn't going to ask that…'

'But I'll tell you. All you have to do is to do the covering paperwork for the Special Orders for these Pompadour suites. That's *all.* You need never touch the stuff itself, *or* know anything about how it's worked. Just see to the paperwork as Sales Manager just so that no one at *all* in your office can fault you.'

'But – how…?'

'That's up to you. Look back and see how Jason did it.'

'And what if I refuse. What if I go to the police right now?'

The smile faded again from Lanaghan's face and his expression grew ugly. 'Where would that get you? This is part of a big organization throughout the country. Your brother was only a link man. That's the only part we want you to play. Just the paperwork and collect your cut once every month.'

Ben remembered Jason's visits to Lanaghan's shop with him. And he'd never thought there was anything out of the ordinary about it. Jason had used him, his own brother as a cover. Lanaghan's next words confirmed Ben's suspicion.

'Your brother was careful to mind didn't get promotion to another area. He wanted you on this area. He said you'd never twig anything and he used to collect his cut and also take another Special Order when he visited with you on your rounds.'

Ben felt a surge of bitterness. Jason had cheated him. He had thought Ben so thick that he would never see what was going on under his nose. And what galled Ben the most was the realization that Jason had been right!

Ben had suspected nothing.

'If you have any bright ideas about going to the police,' Lanaghan was saying with cold deliberation, 'there are plenty of people ready to perjure themselves. Those junkies out there will do anything for a free fix. And what about your brother? Everything would come out, wouldn't it? His part in it, and with false testimony against you, you'd have a devil of a job proving your own innocence, especially now you're in debt. And then,' there was malice in his tone, 'there's your little family. Oh nasty things can happen...'

Ben glanced up at Lanaghan. He felt rage and hatred rising up within him. He was trapped and he knew it. Trapped because of his twin brother's involvement. Trapped because his infatuation for Chloe had led him into debt and to borrow money. Trapped by Lanaghan's blackmail and threats.

With fingers which shook, more from rage than from fear now, Ben lit a cigarette – his fiftieth that day.

'You're a swine, Lanaghan. I'd like to dance at your funeral!'

The words seemed to come out of the blue and they seemed to have a vaguely familiar ring.

Chapter Seven

Ben was surprised how simple it was to make out the bogus paperwork so that no one in the Sales Office, not even the eagle-eyed Jones, could fault it. If he shut his mind to what that paperwork really meant, what was behind it, Ben could find a curious satisfaction in hoodwinking the supercilious Jones. After a few weeks, he became hardened to the fact, but occasionally he would wake up in the middle of the night in a cold sweat from a nightmare where thousands of little white envelopes were fluttering about him, where hippies with outstretched arms were chasing him, and where Lanaghan stood by laughing at him.

But by day Ben's outward appearance became more assured. On the golf course his prowess was in no doubt, and Mr Charlesworth let him know that the Board of Directors were satisfied with him in his new job as Sales Manager.

'Knew you could handle it. Always thought so,' his gravelly voice rumbled. 'Like your brother. Stands to reason. Twins, and all that. Ar-humph! Better find that blasted golf ball now. In the rough, was it?'

Every month Ben visited Lanaghan to collect his cut – or rather to have it deducted from the debt he owed Lanaghan. Ben kept a list of the dates on which the repayment was made deducting it from the original debt. By degrees it seemed to be diminishing.

But then Chloe returned home.

She rang him at the office. 'Ben, that you?'

'Chloe?' At the sound of her voice all the desire and longing he had felt over the weeks of her absence flooded through him.

'I'm home, Ben.'

'Chloe, darling. It's good to hear you. Look, I'll come straight over.'

'Can you?'

'Of course. I'll be right there.'

As Chloe opened the door to him, Ben saw her start, give a small gasp and turn pale.

'Chloe. What's the matter? What is it?'

'Oh Ben!' She gave a small laugh and seemed to recover her composure a little. 'How silly of me. Come in.'

As they moved into the lounge, Ben said again. 'What's the matter? You look as if you'd seen a ghost.'

She turned sharply and looked up at him. 'Why do you say that?'

'You looked at me so – oddly and turned white.'

'Ben – just look at yourself in the mirror.'

'What do you mean?'

'Just look.'

Ben did as she told him. 'Well?'

'Who do you see?'

'What do you mean? Me, of course.'

'*Ben* Winwood?'

Ben looked again. The man looking back at him from the huge mirror was tall with neat, dark hair. His broad shoulders were set straight. His dark suit immaculate.

'The moustache, Ben,' Chloe said softly. 'When did you grow that?'

'About a month ago – just after Christmas.' Ben fingered the pencil-line growth on his upper lip.

'You look just like him now, Ben. *Just like Jason!*'

Ben continued to stare at his reflection.

'That was why I got such a shock when I opened the door to you. You've grown even more like him since I went away. The moustache – just like his – completes it.'

Ben laughed wryly. 'Well, I always wanted

to be like him. So now I've got all I wanted. Or at least,' he turned to face her, his eyes burning with desire, 'almost everything. Chloe…'

He tried to take her in his arms but she twisted away from him. 'Not so fast, Ben. You know what I said before I went away. It still stands. And I also want a car.'

'A *car?*'

'Of course. How can I get about? Into the town to shop without a car. Since Jason smashed our car up…'

'But you didn't have use of that when he was alive. Did you?'

'Of course I did. Except when he went a long distance like the time he went golfing and got himself killed on the way back.'

'Golfing?' Ben sat down opposite her. 'You never said anything about that before. You said you didn't know where he'd been, except that he'd been south.'

'Didn't I? Oh well, I must have forgotten. The shock and everything. The police brought his golf bag back later.'

Now Ben remembered having seen it in the hall, when he had visited Chloe on the day of the inquest. At the time he had thought nothing of it. He realized now that the bag must have only just then been returned. It was out of character for Chloe to leave something untidily cluttering her hall, but at the time the thought had never occurred to him.

'Ben, about the car,' Chloe was saying. 'Jason used a firm's car to go to and from work and for short journeys. He always left me our car.'

'Well, I suppose I could do the same.'

'What – that old car of yours? I'm not driving that. I thought you'd have got a new one by now. Now you've got Jason's job.'

'I've had rather a lot of expense just lately.'

'Well – I need a car to go shopping, to the hairdresser's and so on.'

Ben had a swift mind's eye picture of Jean trailing to the shops a mile from their home, two children in a pushchair and two clutching the pram handle. No car for Jean. Resolutely he blocked out the picture.

'And,' Chloe was saying with firmness. 'If you want me, you've got to leave Jean for good.'

Ben looked at her. Her shining black hair, her smooth skin, tanned to a deep olive colour by the Majorcan sun. Her superb body and shapely legs. God, *if* he wanted her! How he wanted her!

He did some swift calculations in his head. He was managing to meet Lanaghan's repayments on his debt quite easily now, because of the amounts he received for his part in the drug-pushing ring. If he borrowed a further sum from Lanaghan – just once more – it wouldn't be so much more difficult.

'All right,' he stood up. 'It might as well be now. I'll go home and fetch my clothes and tell Jean.'

Chlose smiled triumphantly. 'Oh, just one more thing. Have you got a life insurance?'

'Eh? Er – no.'

'Well, I'd like you to take one out – with *me* as the beneficiary.' She was standing close to him now, her body swaying towards him, but not quite touching him. Hungrily Ben reached out for her. 'Yes, yes,' he murmured hardly understanding to what he was agreeing. 'Anything, anything you say.'

Chloe put her arms round his neck. 'For that, you may kiss me.'

Ben gathered her into his arms and pressed his lips on her mouth, soft and yielding.

'Chloe, Chloe,' he murmured. She laughed and twisted away again. 'That's enough, lover boy, for now.'

Ben slammed the car door and walked up the path towards his house. Then he groaned.

There, on the doorstep, was that religious fellow talking to Jean – the same one who'd come on the day after Jason's death.

Ben swore under his breath. The man turned as Ben approached.

'Ah, good afternoon, sir. We meet again. You're well, I trust? Might I interest you in...'

'Not today, thank you,' Ben said curtly and brushed past the man to enter the house. Jean, her eyes wide, chewed her thumb nail and backed away into the hall. Ben turned to close the door behind him. The caller put his foot between the door and the door jamb. Ben looked down at it, and then glared at him with angry, hostile eyes.

'I said,' Ben repeated slowly, through clenched teeth. 'Not today, thank you.'

'Now look, sir,' the man began placatingly, but not removing his foot.

Ben drew the door open a few inches more and then slammed it viciously against the man's foot. He let out a yell of pain, and dropped his case, leaflets spilling out all over the porch. The foot now removed, Ben slammed the door shut.

'Ben, how could you? You've hurt him.' Tears brimmed in Jean's eyes and she rushed forward to open the door.

Ben caught hold of her wrist roughly. 'Leave it!' he said harshly.

For a long moment Jean gazed up into his face, a mixture of amazement and fear in her eyes. Then gradually she stopped resisting him, and Ben relaxed his hold. He turned away and went into the lounge.

Toys were scattered everywhere. A pile of magazines and newspapers lay on the settee, Jean's knitting in one of the chairs, a pile of unmended socks in the other.

'God – can't you ever tidy this place up, Jean. It's like a rubbish tip!'

Jean stood watching him, her hair untidy as ever, her nose shiny, her dress spattered with baby food, a defeated, helpless look in her tear-filled eyes.

With brutal abruptness Ben said, 'I'm leaving you. I'm going tonight – now.'

Jean gasped. The colour drained from her face and she clasped and unclasped her hands.

'To – *her*?'

'Of course.'

Jean began to cry, great tearing sobs.

'Oh Lord,' said Ben unkindly, 'now the waterworks. I'm getting the full treatment and no mistake.'

After several minutes the first storm of

Jean's weeping abated but every so often she hiccoughed like a child who cries itself to sleep after being sent to bed by an irate parent.

'I don't know how (hic) I'm going to (hic) cope,' she said, biting at her fingernails as if she would tear the flesh from the bone in her anguish. 'What'll I do when things go wrong? Who can I ask for (hic) advice? And what about the (hic) children? They need a father. Oh Ben, we *need* you, Chloe doesn't. I know I'm not (hic) pretty or smart and – I've always known I was only second-best, but I thought we were a happy family. The children love you. And – and I (hic) love you, Ben.' The tears spilled over again.

Ben got up in agitation. 'For God's sake, Jean, shut up! Have you no pride? I expected rages, but not this – this pathetic *begging.*'

Her eyes, swimming with tears, looked up at him, surprise momentarily driving away some of her misery. 'Ben – you – you've never spoken to me like that before. What's got into you?' She frowned slightly and shook her head slowly. 'I don't understand what has happened to you, Ben. I can't begin to. All I know is – you're not the man I married, not the kind, gentle twin, the one who believed himself a failure. He wasn't to me. He was the one I loved – not his conceited, clever brother. You're just like Jason now, Ben. I don't know how it's happened. I'm no psychiatrist, but I suppose it's got something to do with you being twins. Maybe it's always been there in you, but it needed Jason out of the way before it showed up in you. The only other explanation is – rather uncanny – and frightening. I always loved you, Ben, as you were. But I think perhaps I lost you months ago – not to Chloe, but when Jason died.'

She stood up suddenly and faced him with renewed spirit. 'It wasn't Jason who died in that car crash, it was Ben! Jason, somehow, lives on in your body. He's taken you over, Ben. In everything, even so far that you must bed his *wife!* You can go, I don't want you as you are now. I only ever wanted *Ben.'* More gently, she added, with a little more of her characteristic hesitancy, 'if you ever want to come back, just remember this, I'll welcome you with open arms as Ben – the old Ben. But not as you are now. I don't want to be married to *Jason* Winwood.'

Ben did not answer. He merely turned and left the room. Upstairs he threw some of his clothes into a suitcase. As he reached the top step of the stairs on his way down again, the door of the boys' bedroom opened, at first just a crack and then, suddenly, wider.

Julian stood there blinking in the bright light, his hair tousled, his pyjamas a size too big. They'll grow into them, Jean always said, over all the clothes she bought for the children. Why, oh why, Ben thought irrationally, can't she just once buy the kids' clothes to fit?

'You going 'way, Daddy?' Julian's bottom lip, young and tender, quivered.

'Er,' Ben paused, feeling like a burglar caught in the act of stealing the silver. 'Er, yes, just – er – for a while.'

'How long will you be 'way?'

'I don't know – exactly.'

'Why don't you know?'

Ben felt irritation rising. Sharply he snapped, 'Go back to bed, Julian, at once.'

'But, when…?'

'Bed!' roared Ben and Julian scuttled back into the room banging the door behind him. A second later a loud wail arose from Gabrielle in the next room and at the same moment Jean appeared at the foot of the stairs. 'That's right. Take it out on the kids.' She ran upstairs, brushed past him and disappeared into the baby's room.

Ben ran lightly downstairs and left the house, banging the front door behind him as a parting shot.

He threw his suitcase on to the back seat of the car and got into the driving seat. He lit a cigarette, started the car and then drove off with a screech of his tyres.

He was now smoking sixty cigarettes a day.

Chapter Eight

Chloe seemed quite surprised when Ben turned up again on her doorstep complete with suitcase.

'I didn't expect you back – so soon.'

'I said I was coming,' Ben replied shortly.

'I – didn't think you'd *really* do it.'

'What?'

'Leave her.'

Ben said, a little crossly, still smarting from the unpleasant scene with Jean. 'Then you were wrong, weren't you?'

'You mean you've really come to stay?'

'Yes.'

'Oh.' Chloe appeared to be thinking hard.

'What's the matter? Changed your mind now you've got what you wanted?'

Chloe's red lips parted in a slight gasp of surprise. Then suddenly she smiled. 'You're even getting to talk like him.' She turned on her heel. 'I'll make some coffee.'

Ben felt like a nervous bridegroom on his wedding night. For so long his desire for Chloe had been growing, driving all other thoughts from his mind. And now she was within his grasp. Or almost.

As she set the coffee tray down on the low table, Chloe said, 'Of course, you haven't really completed all your side of the bargain yet.'

'What do you mean?'

'The car.'

'That was only mentioned since you came back from Majorca – today.'

'No, I did tell you before. All right, Ben. I give in. But you do promise to get me a car?'

'All right, all right,' Ben said tetchily.

Later that night Ben followed Chloe up the stairs, his eyes upon the perfectly shaped calves of her legs, her slim ankles, the shining heels of her patent shoes.

Excitement rose within him. This was the culmination of his dreams, of his desires.

Some dream! Some desire! Some culmination! It had been a complete failure. Ben rolled over, away from Chloe and sat up on the side of the bed. He reached for his jacket and fumbled in the pocket for his cigarette case and lighter.

He inhaled the smoke deeply and continued to sit there, naked, on the side of the bed, his back to Chloe.

'I don't like you smoking in the bedroom,' Chloe said, but Ben did not appear to have heard.

She had been like an ice-berg. He had been aware all the time of her distaste of the whole business. He could not stop himself, comparing her with Jean – plain, untidy, worrisome Jean, but warm, loving Jean.

'I used to tell Jason, time and again not to smoke up here,' Chloe was saying, and then added, when Ben said nothing and did nothing to extinguish the cigarette. 'And he took no notice either.'

So that, Ben thought with sudden bitterness, was why Chloe had insisted he left Jean entirely before she gave way to his ardent advances. She had known it would be like this and she had guessed that, afterwards, he'd go flitting right back to little Jean. But that wouldn't have suited her plans. So she had made him burn his bridges before he found out what she was really like behind all those coy, flirtatious looks and chic appearance.

She needed him all right! But not in the way he wanted her. She wanted a man to dandle, to bring home a fat wage packet, to keep her 'in the manner to which she had become accustomed'.

Poor old Jason! For the very first time in his life, Ben felt genuine pity for his brother. And then, suddenly, he thought, and now it's poor old Ben! He felt the strands of the web tightening about him. He had left his wife and children. He'd come to live with this beautiful, voluptuous woman who turned out to be cold and unresponsive. He'd become Sales Manager with heavy responsibilities. He had got into debt – because of Chloe – and in so doing had become involved in criminal activities. It all seemed like some dream which had suddenly turned into a horrible nightmare. He was certainly no longer, easy-going, shambling Ben Winwood, the failure. He was someone entirely different.

Ben stubbed out his half-smoked cigarette in the ashtray on the bedside table in angry frustration. He sat looking at the crumpled stub of the cigarette in the light from the bedside lamp.

How often had he seen Jason do just that – stub out a half-smoked cigarette – not long before he died?

By now Chloe was sitting at the dressing-table brushing her dark hair, a long, flowing negligee draped about her lovely body, as if everything were perfectly normal.

Probably it was – for her, thought Ben, wryly. No doubt she didn't think there was anything amiss. He lay back in the bed staring at the ceiling. What a mess he had got himself into. Wherever could it all lead to from here?

His job as Sales Manager was becoming almost routine now, and that, at least, lent an air of normality to the upheaval in his personal life. In the cold light of the following day, Ben rethought, perhaps it was his fault. Perhaps Chloe just needed time. Perhaps things would improve. Perhaps she was still holding herself back a bit until he got her that car. Maybe then she would come to him lovingly, generously.

But in his heart he knew it would not be so.

As Ben shaved in the bathroom the following morning, he was surprised to hear the sound of a vacuum cleaner humming from the lounge downstairs. Surely Chloe, who minutes ago had been sound asleep in bed, had not risen and rushed downstairs to start her housework?

The sound of singing, somewhat off-key, greeted him as he went downstairs, and as he opened the door of the lounge, the noise met him with force. A small, rotund woman, fifty odd, Ben guessed, in a red nylon overall, her grey hair drawn back into a tight bun at the back of her head, was gaily pushing a vacuum cleaner backwards and forwards across the carpet. Turning, she saw Ben standing in the doorway and jumped visibly, dropping the handle of the vacuum. Her singing stopped abruptly, her mouth open, her eyes wide.

Ben moved forward and switched off the noisy machine.

'Lawks, you fair gave me a turn. I thought it was...' she stopped mid-sentence and glared at him. 'And 'oo might you be, may I hask?'

'I was just about to ask you the same question,' Ben replied drily.

'I'm Mrs Phillips. Mrs Winwood's daily, that's who *I* am.' There was pride in the woman's voice as if her explanation verified her right to be there.

'I didn't know she had a daily.'

'Oh lawks, yes!' Mrs Phillips laughed raucously. 'You wouldn't expect a lady like Mrs Winwood to keep a great place like this right 'erself, would you?'

'I – suppose not,' murmured Ben, and unaccountably a picture rose in his mind of Jean, battling single-handed to care for four children and an equally large house.

So often he had made comparisons between Jean and Chloe and their respective houses, with Chloe always winning hands down. Now he saw what a handicap Jean had had against Chloe.

In his frenzied haste to possess Chloe whatever the cost, Ben had entirely miscalculated just what it *would* cost him. He had to send a fair amount of money each month to Jean, and now, of course, Chloe demanded that he pay all her household expenses since it was now his home. Plus, of course, a new car for her.

He went to see Lanaghan one evening, again stepping over the sprawling hippies who seemed to congregate in the alcove nearly every night. There were about ten of them, all long-haired. In the shadows Ben could not distinguish between the girls and the boys. All wore dirty jeans and khaki anoraks. Some carried bundles or rucksacks. Ben imagined they were the sort often described as 'of no fixed abode'.

Lanaghan opened the door and pulled him inside. His eyes were wide and bulging with fear. 'Have they got a look-out posted?' Lanaghan hissed nodding towards the hippies.

'How should I know? What's up?'

'The police have been sniffing round.'

'Here?'

'They came and moved them all on last night, but, of course, they all drifted back after the fuzz had gone.' Beads of sweat were standing on the fat man's shining forehead. He glanced at Ben sharply. 'You haven't been shooting your mouth off, have you?'

'Of course not,' Ben said impatiently.

'You sure?' Lanaghan was none too convinced.

Ben spread his hands in a gesture of innocence. 'It's hardly likely since I've come to see if I can increase my loan.'

Lanaghan passed his hand across his forehead in relief. 'Perhaps it's nothing. Just coincidence. It's a risky business.'

'Yes,' Ben agreed grimly, 'it is.'

'What's this about another loan?'

Ben sighed heavily. He detested having to ask another favour of this man. He'd wracked his brains to think of another – any other – way out. But there was none if he was to keep Chloe. God only knew why he wanted to keep her now – but he did. He still desired her, still hoped her coldness would pass.

'I need another fifteen hundred.'

Lanaghan's eyebrows, pale insignificant lines, rose a fraction. His eyes glittered with triumph, then he smiled. 'Of course, my dear chap, anything to oblige. What I usually do in this sort of case, is to add the additional amount to the amount still left outstanding, and begin again so to speak.' He fished a black, dog-eared notebook from his pocket and thumbed through it. 'Let's see. Ah yes, here we are. That'll make it seventeen fifty to start off again.'

'Seventeen fifty! But I've been paying off a lot more than that. I thought the original five hundred was about clear now.'

'No. That's what you still owe me.'

Ben wanted to walk out of the shop, tell Lanaghan to forget the whole thing, but the words would not come. He stood there unable to utter a word, unable to move, to escape from this man's clutches. In his confusion, he couldn't even argue against Lanaghan's calculations. He couldn't remember the details of the agreement on the original loan – and, even so, as there had, of course, been nothing in writing, what could he prove anyway? Ben had an uncomfortable feeling that Lanaghan was extracting far more in repayments from him than he had originally said. He was certainly caught in the jaws of a proper 'loan shark' and no mistake!

'Do you want it now – in cash?'

'Cash? Well,' Ben hesitated. He didn't fancy walking out past all those hippy types with fifteen hundred pounds on him. 'Couldn't you make it a cheque?'

'Sorry, old chap. All cash transactions.' Lanaghan tapped the side of his nose with his forefinger. 'Can't have the banks and the income tax man getting too interested now can I?'

'All right, I'll take it in cash then.'

As Ben negotiated his way back to his car, stepping carefully over the sprawling, twitching legs of the waiting drug addicts, he felt someone grasp his arm.

''Ow much longer is 'ee goin' to keep us waiting? Look, this kid 'ere, is in a bad way. She must have a fix soon, or...'

Ben glanced down at the girl. She was fair and could have been quite pretty, though her hair was long, dirty and ill-kept. Her face was distorted by the pain she was suffering. She was writhing on the floor, clutching her leg from time to time and muttering. 'Oh God, Oh God.' Suddenly, she began to retch on the floor and Ben turned away quickly. Panic surged up in him. He pulled his arm free from the young man's grasp and began to run. Tripping over someone's legs, he fell heavily, sprawling in an ungainly position on the top of several other sprawling bodies. Hands reached up to push him off, to lift him up on to his feet.

'Watch it, mate.'

'Look out!'

''Ere, Grandad, you'll be 'urting yerself.'

More hands brushed his clothes. The young man who had grabbed him by the arm, stood before him grinning in the half-light. 'There now, Dad. You'll be all right. Take it steady.'

Ben pushed him aside and hurried away. With trembling fingers he opened the car door and got in. He lit a cigarette to calm himself, and then drove away, his tyres squealing. He couldn't get away from Lanaghan's shop and all its secrets fast enough.

It wasn't until he got home to Chloe's house that he discovered the money in his inside pocket – all fifteen hundred pounds – had gone.

Ben groaned aloud, flopped down on to the settee and dropped his head into his hands.

'What is it?' Chloe said.

For several minutes he did not answer. He could not.

'What is it, Ben?' she said again, more sharply. 'Are you ill?'

'Money, some money. It's been stolen.'

'What do you mean – stolen? Ben, you're not making any sense.'

'I had some money on me. Quite a lot. Someone's picked it out my pocket.'

'But how on earth could they do that?'

'I...' Ben stopped. He didn't want to tell Chloe about Lanaghan, about the drug addicts and the activities in which he had become involved. It was best that she knew nothing.

He waved her away with a gesture of impatience. 'Don't worry about it. I'll – see to it.'

Chloe pouted petulantly. 'I suppose you'll say next it was the money for my car. That you can't get me one now.'

Ben swung round. 'How did you know?'

Chloe looked up at him, her eyes narrowing. 'I didn't. But I know you men. Jason was like that. If there was anything I particularly wanted, he always had some excuse ready.'

'It isn't an excuse, it's the truth.'

'Expect me to believe that?' she said scathingly. 'You must think I'm dumb!'

'No,' Ben said thoughtfully. 'No – you're

certainly not that.'

He dialled Lanaghan's number. If he was still there, he might be able to recover the money from the person who'd taken it. The ringing tone sounded in his ear and went on and on and on. Lanaghan had either left or was not answering a call late at night, after closing time, in case it was a trap.

There was nothing more Ben could do. There was no point in going back. The one who'd taken it would be far away by now. He couldn't even go to the police!

The following morning he rang Lanaghan from his office. 'Look, you know what I came about last night.'

'Yes,' replied Lanaghan guardedly.

'Well, as I was leaving, it was nicked from my pocket.'

'Really? I *am* sorry, old chap.' There was sarcasm in Lanaghan's tone but no real surprise.

'Is there anything you can do? I mean, you know those people.'

Lanaghan laughed softly. 'Know them? I don't know them. I only do business with them.'

'But...'

'Look,' Lanaghan's tone was less jovial, 'there's nothing I can do. It's your hard luck.

161

You should take better care of your – possessions.'

The 'phone clicked and the dialling tone buzzed in Ben's ear. Lanaghan had rung off. Then there was another click, nearer, as if an extension 'phone had been carefully replaced.

Ben sat for a long time without doing anything. Just staring straight ahead, seeing nothing of his surroundings. Not the huge, polished desk with its telephones and files stacked neatly on one side. Nor the pile of mail on his blotter, placed there ready opened and sorted, the letters attached to previous relevant correspondence where necessary, by his efficient secretary. He saw only Chloe's face, ever-demanding, or Lanaghan's evil, smiling face.

Abstractedly, he pulled a blank sheet of paper from one of the drawers in his desk and reached for his pen. He began to make a list of dates on the right-hand side – the dates on which he had repaid Lanaghan money. The second column by each date he wrote the amount he had paid off. The third column he headed with the original sum borrowed and deducted the amount paid each time to give a decreasing total. Then he added on, in the third column, the sum of fifteen hundred –

the money he had borrowed from Lanaghan and had had stolen. The last figure in the third column now swelled alarmingly.

When he had finished writing he sat staring at the list in front of him. It looked very familiar – the layout of dates and two columns of figures.

He had seen such a list somewhere before.

But the relevant door in his memory refused to open, and he could not think where or when he had read such a list previously. Of course, now his every working day was filled with list upon list of Sales figures. Perhaps his mind was confusing the issue. Somehow, the eerie feeling that this had all happened before persisted.

Ben continued to stare at the last figure in the third column, wondering how he could raise yet more cash whilst still trying to pay his debt off.

Of course! Chloe's insurance money. Why hadn't he thought of that before instead of borrowing again from Lanaghan? Each time he mentioned it to her, she had said the firm were still refusing to pay out. He lifted the receiver and asked his secretary to put a call through to the insurance company with whom Jason had dealt.

'Get me someone in authority, Miss

Peebles. I don't want to mess about with small fry.'

'No, Mr Winwood. Certainly, Mr Winwood,' came Miss Peebles' plum-filled tones. A few minutes later she rang back. 'I have a Mr Kinross on the line, Mr Winwood. He is a senior member of the personnel.'

'Right.'

Briefly, Ben explained who he was. 'My brother took out a policy with your firm, and was killed about four months later. I understand from Mrs Chloe Winwood, his widow, that you are withholding payment. I've been helping her sort out my brother's affairs, you understand, and it seemed about time *I* spoke to you about this.' Ben's tone was brusque and left little room for a chance of excuses from the man on the other end of the line.

'What was your brother's full name, Mr Winwood?'

'Jason Winwood.'

'And the date of his death?'

'June thirteenth last.'

'Right, sir. I'll check immediately.' There was a clattering in Ben's ear as Kinross put the receiver down. Several minutes ticked by then Kinross's voice sounded again in Ben's ear.

'Sorry to keep you so long, Mr Winwood, but your call has raised a bit of a query on this one and I had to double check. Anyway, I now have the facts.' He cleared his throat busily. Ben cast his eyes to the ceiling in impatience.

'It seems we did withhold payment for a few weeks, Mr Winwood, as your brother had only paid one premium.'

'He couldn't help getting killed so quickly afterwards, could he?' Ben said tersely.

'No, no, of course not. Quite so,' Kinross replied hurriedly, placatingly. 'But I'm sure you will appreciate that in such circumstances – the car accident and everything – we have to be sure the claim is genuine.'

'And?'

'Well, we satisfied ourselves of that fact, Mr Winwood, and payment was made to Mrs Chloe Winwood by cheque dated thirtieth of August for an amount of seven thousand five hundred pounds.'

Ben nearly dropped the receiver he held.

Chloe had been paid.

'But ... but – um,' he faltered for a moment and tried to think quickly. 'Could the cheque have got lost in the post?'

'Oh no. It was presented less than a week after we posted it, Mr Winwood. Mrs

165

Winwood certainly received the money, I do assure you.'

'I see,' Ben added stiffly, embarrassed by his faux pas. 'I'm very sorry to have troubled you.'

'No trouble, sir, glad to be of assistance. Goodbye.'

Again just as he replaced the receiver, Ben heard another click, but paid little attention to it. His thoughts were elsewhere. So, Chloe had been paid the insurance money – and a large amount – and all this time had lied to him in order to extract even more from him.

The thirtieth of August, Kinross had said. And she'd left for Majorca at the end of September. She hadn't really needed any of the money he had borrowed from Lanaghan. He had got himself into such straits just to satisfy Chloe's greed.

Ben felt cheated and humiliated. And now there was the second lot of money he had borrowed from Lanaghan to be paid back, money which he had had stolen and could do nothing to retrieve.

What an unholy mess he'd landed himself in. He looked about him. The plush furniture, the deep-piled carpet, all symbols of his rise in position, in status.

Suddenly, the whole thing had turned sour.

Ben sat at his executive desk surrounded by papers, letters, telephones. He stubbed out his half-smoked cigarette, hardly aware of his actions. His fingers searched automatically in his pocket for his cigarette case and lighter to light another one.

There was a knock at his office door.

'Come in.'

Jones came in, a sheaf of papers in his hand. 'Can you spare a moment?' Jones never called him by name, nor did he ever add a 'please' or 'thank you'.

Automatically Ben said, 'Yes'.

The sheaf of papers Jones carried landed on Ben's desk in front of him.

'There's something funny about these orders.'

There was a pause. Ben attempted to drag his wandering thoughts back to concentrate on the papers in front of him. 'Oh. In what way?'

'They're all "Specials" for a Pompadour suite in some ridiculous colour called cerise.'

Ben felt the sweat prickle the back of his neck. He inhaled deeply on his cigarette.

Surprisingly, his voice, when he spoke again, was remarkably calm. 'What about them?'

'The suite itself is authentic, but the material is not in the pattern swatch.'

'That's why they're called "Specials",' Ben said with deliberate mildness.

Jones put his hands flat on the desk and leant forward, towering over the seated Ben. 'All the orders are for one shop. Lanaghan, in Melchester High Street. Why?'

Ben shrugged. 'He must find it a good seller.'

'Then why, may I ask, has it not been included in the pattern swatch as a regular colour choice?'

Ben felt his fingers tremble slightly, but he managed to answer casually enough. 'I really couldn't tell you.'

'Isn't it part of your job to introduce new ideas to boost sales?'

Ben glanced up at Jones's sly face. So his assistant had found the opportunity he had been waiting for. He had cornered Ben. Immediately, Ben wondered if it had been Jones listening in on an extension to his conversation with Lanaghan earlier that morning.

Ben nodded in dismissal. 'Leave it with me. I'll look into it.'

'But don't you think...?'

'I said,' Ben muttered through clenched teeth. 'I'll look into it.'

As the door closed behind Jones, Ben felt the waves of fear wash over him. Could the snooping, sneaking Jones be on to something? Ben glanced through the orders which covered the 'Specials'. Each one was signed by Ben personally. Condemnation by his own hand! He wouldn't put it past Jones to take the matter to Petersen or even to Mr Charlesworth, if he could make trouble for Ben. But did Jones know just what trouble it would cause?

Ben felt the web tightening about him.

For four weeks the problem of Jones and the Special Orders nagged at Ben. Then with a blinding flash he saw a way out.

Dismiss his Assistant Manager!

But on what grounds? The man was good at his work – a darn sight too good! Perhaps Ben could catch Jones out on something and use it as an excuse to sack him. Reluctantly Ben had to admit to himself that this would be highly unlikely. Jones was a clever operator. How do you sack a man without a legitimate reason? You made one. But how?

Ben had no experience of having to sack anyone, or of even wanting to do so. Then he remembered.

Jason had sacked his Assistant Manager three weeks before he died? Vaguely, Ben wondered if it could have been for the same reason that he now wished to dismiss his assistant. Jason had, in exactly the same way, for Ben had copied his modus operandi, issued the orders to cover the Specials for Lanaghan. Perhaps his assistant too had begun to ask awkward questions.

How had Jason dealt with the problem? Ben stayed late at the office that night and after all the staff had left, including Jones, Ben began leafing through the filing cabinet. There must be some paperwork which dealt with the previous Assistant Manager's dismissal.

'Let's see, three weeks before Jason's death,' Ben muttered, leafing through his diary. 'What date would that be. About mid-May.'

He opened the filing cabinet on personnel. After several minutes searching, he found what he was looking for. A letter from Jason addressed to George Reynolds, Assistant Sales Manager dated 21st May. 'That's funny,' murmured Ben. 'Day after tomorrow, it'll be a year to the day.'

'Following our recent conversation,' Ben

read, 'and with Mr Petersen's agreement, I hereby confirm that by mutual consent, your services are no longer required by Charlesworth Ltd...'

The letter went on to give details of salary due, holiday pay and so on.

'So Petersen knew about it,' Ben murmured. He read the letter through again, but it still gave no indication as to the reason Jason had dismissed Reynolds. Ben could not imagine that he and Jones would come to 'mutual consent'.

He wondered whether Petersen would be able to give him any idea as to how Jason had got rid of Reynolds and why? But Ben would have to be careful or Petersen too might begin to inquire into the 'Special Orders'. However, Ben decided that since he was taking enough risks already one way and another, one more wouldn't make any difference.

He would see Petersen in the morning.

'Come in, come in, Winwood. Sit down. What can I do for you?'

'Well, Mr Petersen, it's a little delicate. You remember my brother dismissed his Sales Manager about three weeks before his death?'

Petersen seemed to start and hesitate slightly before he said, 'Yes. What of it?'

'Do you know why he dismissed the man?'

Petersen appeared to think for a moment or two, leaning back in his swivel chair swinging gently from side to side. 'I believe the man became – er – how shall I put it? Awkward to work with. He started – questioning your brother's authority. Delving into – er – orders your brother initiated and dealt with personally. It was obvious that they couldn't work together so your brother,' Petersen spread his hands in the air, 'asked him to leave.'

It sounded so similar to the circumstances in which Ben now found himself, it was uncanny. Petersen was eyeing Ben with a piercing shrewdness which Ben found disconcerting.

'Having trouble with *your* man?'

There was no point in trying to deceive Petersen. If Ben wanted to be rid of Jones, Petersen would have to know, would have to agree, in fact.

'Yes. To be honest, ever since the appointment was made he's been trying to – to catch me out, for want of a better phrase. I've felt it. He doesn't work with me, but against me.' Ben sighed. 'Point is, he's good

172

at his job.'

Petersen leant forward, his arms on his desk. 'What exactly is he trying to do?'

Ben took a deep breath. He'd have to tell Petersen too much to explain. Just about the Specials, just what was on the paperwork for all to see anyway. No need to say any more.

'There's a particular suite – the Pompadour – one of our customers has it made up in a special material – one which isn't in the pattern swatch. This is a long-standing arrangement since Jason's time. This – customer has an outlet for that particular colour so – we oblige him.'

Petersen nodded. 'I know about it.'

Ben looked up quickly. 'You do?' For a moment he felt the fear creeping up his scalp. But Petersen leaned back in his chair smiling. 'Oh yes, Lanaghan has been a good customer for years. It's something we don't mind doing occasionally. What's the trouble then?'

'Jones thinks if this – Lanaghan can sell it so well, the colour ought to be included as a regular pattern choice.'

'Does he indeed?' Petersen's eyes narrowed. 'And – what – do you – think?' Each word was spoken with measured deliberation.

'I don't think it would be a good seller generally.'

Again Petersen smiled. 'No, I quite agree, my dear fellow.'

There was a pause whilst the two men eyed each other. Ben had the strange feeling that perhaps Petersen knew more than he was admitting. That they both knew what it was all about, but neither would put it into words.

'What do you propose to do about Mr Jones?'

'I – don't know.'

'May I suggest,' Petersen said smoothly. 'That you say to him that the decision about the Special Orders is yours and yours alone. If he does not feel able to co-operate with you entirely in all matters of the Company's policy, then he had better leave.'

Ben rose. 'Thank you, Mr Petersen. You've been most helpful, most helpful.'

'Any time, my dear fellow, any time.'

As Ben left his office, Mr Petersen leant back in his chair, his elbows resting on the arms of the chair, his hands fingertips to fingertips, smiling smugly.

Ben repeated Petersen's words almost verbatim to the astonished Jones. When he had finished Jones, his temper flaring, said, 'Then I will go. I don't want to work with a crook any longer.'

Ben sprang to his feet. 'What the hell do you mean?'

Jones pointed an accusing finger at Ben. 'There's something funny about those Special Orders. Why that suite, why that colour? We don't do it for anybody else in the whole of our area – only Lanaghan. It's Special all right. What I'd like to know is – why?'

'Lanaghan is an old customer. We don't mind doing this sort of thing occasionally.'

'Oh, don't we? How very accommodating of us.' Jones's tone was heavy with sarcasm.

'You had better leave at once,' Ben said, 'there's no point in your staying here any longer.'

'All right, I'm going. But you watch it, Winwood. You'll come to a nasty end, you will.'

The door slammed and Jones was gone.

With shaking fingers Ben stubbed out one half-smoked cigarette and immediately lit another.

His eightieth that day.

Chapter Nine

The following week the headline of the *Melchester Chronicle* hit him like a physical blow.

'Girl drug addict found dead in Melchester High Street.'

As Ben read the report further he felt sick with revulsion and shame. It appeared that the girl had been found in the alcove of Lanaghan's shop, and, went on the relentless print, although the post-mortem was still to be held, it was a known fact that the girl was an addict and it was a foregone conclusion that drugs had, in some way, caused her death.

Ben crumpled the paper fiercely. He had helped to kill that girl almost as if he had strangled her. A picture of his own daughters floated before his eyes. Laughing, dancing girls, running, jumping, playing, climbing up him, hugging him, loving him.

God, how he missed them!

He looked back at the paper he held in his hands. *In a few years' time it could be his daughter dying in the street — because of what he, Ben Winwood, was doing now.*

By the time he had reached his office, his fear had given way to anger, a smouldering rage against Lanaghan who had involved him in this awful business. He dialled Lanaghan's number.

'Lanaghan? Have you seen this morning's paper?'

Lanaghan's tone was guarded. 'Yes.'

'Look, Lanaghan,' Ben's voice was barely controlled. 'I want out. I want no more to do with – with this filthy business...'

Lanaghan's voice came smoothly over the line. 'I'm sorry, sir, I can't attend to your query now. *I have the police with me.* Perhaps you would care to ring me again, or better still, call in the shop later. You will, thank you. Goodbye.' The line went dead.

'Damn him!' Ben cursed and slammed his receiver down.

In the alcove to the shop that night there were no hippies crowding the doorway. Ben knocked on the glass door and waited.

Lanaghan, his eyes darting about as if he expected someone to jump out of the shadows at him, opened it. Serve him right if someone did, Ben thought viciously, the mealy-mouthed rat!

'I want out,' Ben said before the door was scarcely shut behind him.

'Not so fast, my friend, not so fast.'

'That girl,' Ben pointed towards the door, 'who died out there. Don't you care? Don't you give a damn?'

Lanaghan shrugged. 'I don't make them take the stuff.'

'No, but you provide it.'

'And you help me get it.'

'I know, and that's the part I like least of all. I want no further part in it.'

'And just how are you going to pay back the money you owe me?'

'I'm not.'

'Oh-ho, yes you are.'

'I'm not. I'm going to the police. I'm going to tell them all about...'

Lanaghan's pudgy hands closed on Ben's arm in a vice-like grip. 'I said, not so fast. You're living with Jason's widow, aren't you?'

'How...?'

Lanaghan smiled that sickly, sarcastic smirk. 'You like her, don't you? You think she's a good-looker, don't you? You're right, she is. You left your family for her so obviously it's her you care most about.' Ben had sense enough to keep quiet about the failure of his affair with Chloe. There was an ominous pause before Lanaghan added. 'It would be such a pity if that beautiful face was to – er – meet with a little accident, wouldn't it?'

'Are you threatening me?'

Lanaghan merely continued to smile. 'You've no choice, Winwood. Either you be a good boy, or else...'

Ben clenched and unclenched his fists in frustrated rage. He jerked his arm free of Lanaghan's grasp, turned and dragged open the shop door. He turned back and shook his fist at Lanaghan. 'I'll dance at your funeral yet, Lanaghan.'

The glass door shook as he slammed it behind him.

Lanaghan's eyes narrowed and he walked into his office, picked up the 'phone and dialled.

'Lanaghan here. Winwood's just been here. He's getting – awkward. *Just like his brother did.* You'll have to put the frighteners on him too.'

There was a pause.

'This business in the paper. It's got him scared.'

Another pause.

'Well, we'll have to risk that. You'll have to do something to make sure he keeps his mouth shut.'

It was like a nightmare from which Ben could not wake up. He could not meet his debts, for Lanaghan still insisted he pay off the money he had had stolen. Chloe still nagged him about getting her a car, and as a punishment she refused to sleep with him. Not that that was any great loss, for every time he had made love to her, for him it had been a complete failure.

He began to think more and more of Jean and the children. He missed their smiling faces, their chubby arms about his neck, and strangely, he missed his mother whom he had not visited for months. He began to see that his life as ordinary Ben Winwood, the failure, had been wonderful in comparison to his life now. He'd gone up the ladder, all right, he'd got a top job, but what a lot of worry and fear had come with it.

Ben couldn't remember ever having heard his mother's voice over the telephone, so that when she rang him one Monday morning at the office, it took several moments for him to realize who it was.

'That you, Ben?'

'Er – yes – er…'

'You haven't been for weeks.'

Suddenly, he realized to whom the sharp, clipped tones belonged. 'Oh Mother! Er – no – well…'

'Come tonight.' It was a command not a request.

Ben felt irritation rise within him and was about to retort that he would be working late, when there was a click and the dialling tone sounded in his ear.

His mother had hung up.

When she opened the door to him, he saw she wore her perpetual look of disapproval – especially directed at him. Strangely, and for perhaps the very first time in his life, her expression failed to have any effect upon him. Usually, he quailed at the sight of the slight, yet to him formidable, figure. As he walked behind her into the front room, he towered above her.

Ben realized he was no longer afraid of his mother.

'Well. Why haven't you been to see me recently?'

Ben sprawled, at ease, on the hard sofa. 'Busy. New job. Demanding, you know.'

His mother sniffed contemptuously. 'Huh! Not the *only* thing that's occupying your time the way I hear it.' She glared at him. 'Why have you left Jean and the children?'

'I wondered how long it would be before you heard,' Ben murmured mildly.

'And gone to live with that trollop.'

Ben sat up quickly, the mildness gone in a flash. 'Chloe is not a trollop. She – she's a fine woman.'

'Huh!'

'She was all right for your precious *Jason*. Why is she suddenly no good?'

'Jason didn't leave a wife and four children.'

'No – but he took Chloe from me in the first place. It was me met her first, me she went out with, until he appeared on the scene.'

'Ah, so that's it, is it?' Mrs Winwood actually smiled – a thin, humourless smile, but nonetheless a smile.

'Yes – that's it! All my life,' Ben sprang to his feet, leant over his mother and wagged his forefinger in her face, 'all my life, I've lived in his blasted shadow. He's beaten me at everything. Well, now he's dead. Dead *and buried*. And I'm just beginning to live. And no one – not even you, you old buzzard, is going to spoil it for me. Got it?'

To his amazement, Mrs Winwood's smile broadened. With claw-like fingers, she reached up and patted his cheek.

'That's my boy,' she murmured. 'That's more like my boy!' It was the same gesture and the same words she had so often used to Jason.

Ben straightened. He was not going to be taken in by her soft-soaping *him*. Just because Jason was dead she needn't think she could transfer her affections to him just like that.

Ben moved towards the door. 'I'll dance at your funeral, you old buzzard. Just you wait and see!'

He left, slamming the front door behind him, leaving the stiff-backed figure of Mrs Clementine Winwood sitting bolt upright in her chair, her eyes afire with a new found joy.

Ben was wrong. Jason, her dearest boy, her only love, was not dead.

Jason still lived on in Ben, as she had hoped.

Petersen, meeting Ben in the executive dining-room the next day at lunch-time, put a hand on his shoulder. 'Mr Charlesworth told me to ask you if you'd like to come down to his country estate for a couple of days. A stag do. A golfing weekend on his private golf course. On Wednesday, the tenth June.'

'I don't know. I don't think I can, thanks.'

'Now look, old chap, when Mr Charlesworth invites you, it doesn't do to refuse. Really it doesn't. Besides, you're due for some time off. We know you've been working very hard since you took over as Sales Manager and Mr Charlesworth wants to express his satisfaction with your efforts.'

'Well...' Ben hesitated. It was a tempting invitation. He could get away from everything even if only for a couple of days. No Chloe, no Lanaghan breathing down his neck! Unless Lanaghan was invited too!

'Who would be going?'

'Oh, just Mr Charlesworth, myself, you and – er – perhaps one or two others. I'm not really sure.'

'Would – Lanaghan be going?'

'Why do you ask?'

'No reason, really,' Ben attempted a casual air. 'I just wondered.'

'As a matter of fact, no. He can't leave his shop for that length of time. Doesn't like to leave his assistants for more than the odd day.'

'Then I'd be delighted to accept.'

Ben thought Petersen cast him a strange look but it was gone in a second, and the Managing Director patted him on the shoulder and smiled. 'Good, good. We drive down next Wednesday afternoon and return on the Friday, the twelfth that'll be. Mr Charlesworth has other engagements over the weekend I understand.'

Ben almost stopped in his tracks. Friday, the twelfth of June. That would be a year all but a day since Jason had been killed! On Friday, the thirteenth of June the previous year Jason had died, returning from a golfing expedition.

Ben made the journey in his own car, on his own. He'd been given directions as to how to reach Charlesworth's country estate on the Norfolk coast, and found the drive down south from the Yorkshire moors pleasant and, for once, relaxing. The further he drove from Melchester, the further away he got from all his worries. From Chloe, from Lanaghan, from his work, from his debts, from – his criminal activities.

He found himself wishing that he did not have to return on Friday. *That he need never go back at all.*

Charlesworth's estate, which included his own private eighteen hole golf course, lay on a stretch of coastline not far from the famous Broads. Several times Ben took the wrong turning and found himself amongst quaint Norfolk villages. But eventually he came to the estate. Winding lanes brought him finally to the house, standing on its own, not another building in sight. Between it and the coast stretched a well-kept golf course and beyond that the undulating line of sandhills covered with grass. A cool breeze blew in from the sea. Ben shivered as he got out of the warm interior of his car.

It was late when Ben arrived and though not dark at this time of the year, it was dusk and Ben saw nothing of his host or of Petersen that night. He was shown to his room, with private bathroom, by a manservant whom he presumed to be a butler, though he looked nothing like that particular breed of aristocratic servant. The butler was a big man, with powerful shoulders. He had a craggy, ex-boxer-like face, and his black suit and bow tie ill-suited his bearing.

Tired from the long drive down, and strangely light-headed to have got away, if only for a brief respite, from all his day-to-day worries, Ben fell into the comfortable bed and slept soundly until he was awoken by the return of the butler the following morning, bearing a breakfast tray.

'Thanks – er...' Ben hesitated. The butler paused in the doorway, turned and waited for Ben to continue. 'Where can I find Mr Charlesworth after breakfast?'

'Library.' The door closed behind the butler.

Some butler! Ben thought as he attacked the cereal, eggs and bacon with more appetite than he had had for months.

'Mr Charlesworth would be glad if you would join him in the library, after you have breakfasted, sir,' was the sort of reply Ben would have expected from a well-trained butler. Not 'Library' and a closed door!

'Come in, come in, my dear chap,' Mr Charlesworth moved across the book-lined room to greet Ben. Petersen stood before a huge fireplace carved out of dark wood. He smiled and nodded at Ben.

'Good, good. All ready then? Right.' Charlesworth dressed in typical golfing gear, rubbed his hands together. 'Off we go.'

Ben enjoyed himself. For the first time in months. The fresh air, the green turf, springy beneath his feet, the good food Charlesworth provided. And he won one of the rounds. They played nine holes in the morning and a further eighteen in the afternoon. During the afternoon round, at the seventeenth, Ben chipped a shot to the left of the green.

As the three of them – Ben found there were no other guests other than Petersen and himself – approached the green, Charlesworth and Petersen were well placed on the green, but Ben's golf ball was nowhere to be seen.

'I think it veered off over there,' he said.

Ben felt, rather than saw, Charlesworth and Petersen exchange a glance.

'Ar – hum, well. Ground's boggy over there, old chap. If it's far over, that's it. We'll have to – er – let you have a drop ball, or something,' he finished lamely.

Ben squinted in the direction he thought his ball had gone. 'Boggy, you say? But there's a building over there.'

'Ar – hum,' Charlesworth grunted again. 'Old club house. Don't use it now. Derelict.'

'I'll have a look anyway,' Ben said cheerfully and set off across the grass. He left the smooth grass of the fairway and began searching in the rough for the white ball.

'Doesn't seem at all boggy here,' he murmured, and then stopped suddenly as he found himself teetering on the edge of a deep bunker, and staring down at the upturned face of the butler who seemed to be in the act of digging at the bottom of the sandy bunker. For a moment the two men stared at each other, each surprised to see the other there.

'Seen a golf ball fly this way, old chap?' Ben said breezily, the first to recover from the surprise.

'No.' The man did not move, he just stood stock still, his spade poised to strike the ground.

'Oh – er, don't bother to dig for it, old man,' Ben laughed, attempting a futile joke with the poker-faced manservant. He turned and made his way back towards Charlesworth and Petersen who appeared to be still standing on the very same spot as when he'd left them, watching his every movement.

'Can't find it. I say your butler chappie is digging in a deep bunker over there. Looking for treasure, is he?' Ben laughed loudly.

This time he was fully aware of the glance which passed between Charlesworth and Petersen.

'Ar – hum, you could say that. Come on,

let's get on with it.'

They arrived back at the mansion for a superb dinner at about seven in the evening, and the remainder of the evening was spent in casual chat over drinks and cigars. They never spoke of work, and while the conversation centred mainly on golf and therefore Charlesworth and Petersen seemed to do most of the talking, Ben did not feel excluded from their elite circle. In fact he felt completely at ease in their company, the warmth of the brandy flooded through him, the fire welcoming, the light conversation and ready available cigars lulled him into a sense of security.

It was all too good to last.

Chapter Ten

A bright light was shining in his face and a hand was shaking him roughly by the shoulder.

'What the...?'

'You – up.'

'Wha's the matter?' Ben was heavy with sleep and he couldn't see a thing for that light. He put up his hand to shield his eyes, but it was knocked away again by a blow from a bigger, strong hand.

'Come on, out.'

Ben half-scrambled, was half-dragged, out of bed.

'Get dressed.'

'What's...?'

'Shut up and get dressed.'

'I can't see where my clothes are.'

The light from the powerful torch swung away from his eyes and travelled briefly round the room coming to rest on the neatly folded clothes on a chair and hanging above them from the picture rail, his sports jacket and flannels.

'Make it snappy.'

Wide awake now, Ben dressed. The man laid his torch on the bed. 'Right, turn round.' Ben felt himself twisted round and his arms forced behind his back. Roughly the man tied his wrists together, the harsh cord biting into his flesh. Then a gag was tied about his mouth, so tightly that he thought it would choke him. Lastly a blindfold was fastened over his eyes.

'In case you have any fancy ideas about making a run for it, I'm only a yard behind – with this.'

Ben felt a small, hard object jabbed viciously in the small of his back and knew it to be a revolver.

Ben had thought his life had become a nightmare in Melchester. If that had been a nightmare, then this must be Hell!

'Right, march.' Another vicious jab in the back and Ben marched. Out of the room, down the stairs, across the hall, and out through the front door. As he stumbled blindly forward, his brain began to recover from the initial shock and began to work again.

What the devil was happening to him? And more important how could he get away? They were walking across grass now. It seemed miles Ben stumbled and hobbled. From time to time the gun was jabbed against his spine by way of 'encouragement'. Suddenly Ben felt himself falling, and rolling down and down. When he stopped and tried to scramble to his feet, he felt the sand gritty beneath him. At once he realized where he was. They had been walking across the golf course, and now he had fallen into a bunker. A raucous laugh from his captor greeted Ben's feeble efforts to climb out of the bunker. It was a deep one and difficult to climb out of with his hands behind his back. Time and again Ben slid back and then fell in a heap at the bottom of the bunker. The laughter continued, until Ben decided to lie doggo. The laughter changed to anger.

'Come on, you. Up.'

Ben lay still.

'I said, up.'

Ben did not move.

The shot in the stillness made him almost jump out of the bunker in fright. It hit the ground somewhere close to his head – too close, showering sand into his face.

'I said – up.'

Ben moved quickly, and, to his surprise, found himself on firm ground at the top of the bunker, fear giving him the added impetus required. His fall into the bunker and his struggle to get out had loosened the blindfold and it fell off, though the painful gag was as secure as ever. The June morning was bright, even though he knew it must be very early. He looked about him. They were standing some hundred yards from the disused club house, and the bunker into which Ben had fallen was the same one in which he had seen the butler digging the previous day. He was about to turn round to look at his captor, to see who it was, when again the gun jabbed into his ribs, pushing him towards the derelict building.

The man kicked open the door of the wooden building and pushed Ben inside. It was dark once the door was shut behind them for all the windows had been boarded up. At once a huge light – far bigger than the torchlight – was switched on to shine directly into his eyes. Ben blinked and tried to turn away but his assailant's rough hands pushed him forward and held him facing the light. The man grasped his hair and pulled his head back so that the light, some sort of spotlight, shone full in his face. Ben kept his eyes shut, but even so the light was blinding.

Ben waited – he had no choice. He heard a whispering and a shuffling somewhere beyond the light.

Then came a voice. 'Remove the gag. Now, Winwood. Know why you're here?' The voice seemed familiar but for the moment, in the garish surroundings, Ben couldn't just place it.

'Answer the Boss.' The man holding Ben brought his knee up sharply into Ben's back.

'No – I don't.'

'I hope you're not going to be difficult, Winwood.' Another voice smoother, silkier than the first one.

Then the first man spoke again. Gravelly tones, in short clipped sentences. 'Lanaghan says you're getting awkward. Won't do. You're in this drug business. Up to your neck. No way out. If you try anything…'

The gun was a sharp reminder of the serious reality of this nightmare.

Ben stiffened. He knew that voice, and the other one too. Suddenly he felt an over-whelming rage.

'Turn this bloody light off,' he shouted.

There was a moment's surprised silence before the smooth voice said again, 'Still a little fight left, I see. Dear me!'

'I know who you are,' Ben shouted. 'I'd know that voice anywhere. *Mr Charlesworth.*

And you, Petersen.'

There was a moment's whispering, then Charlesworth said, 'All right. Turn the light out. No point in it now.'

The light was switched off but it was several minutes before Ben could see anything clearly, for stars still danced before his eyes. Then he saw that they were in a large room lit now by a dim light from a single bulb in the centre of the room. Against the walls of the room were stacked chairs and settees. All the same style, all covered in the same material. *Pompadour suites in cerise moquette.* Each settee and some of the chairs had their backs slashed open as Ben had seen Lanaghan do to the one in the attic above the shop.

Then, as Ben's eyes became more accustomed to the ordinary light, his gaze turned towards his captors.

Suddenly his whole world seemed to shatter into a million pieces. His heart lurched and then pounded painfully and his knees almost gave way with shock.

Sitting between Charlesworth and Petersen was...

'Chloe!' He heard himself speak her name in a strangulated whisper.

'Hi there, Ben. Surprise, surprise.'

'You – you're *not* mixed up in this too with – with…' Ben's voice gave out and he made a helpless gesture with his hand towards Petersen and Charlesworth.

Chloe smiled with icy sweetness. 'I have been "involved" right from the start, sweetie.'

'You mean – you mean with Jason.'

'Oh, *before* Jason,' she replied airily.

'Chloe,' Petersen said slowly and deliberately, smiling with a cold, vicious delight in seeing Ben suffer, 'and I are brother and sister…'

'Oh my God!' Ben heard his own hoarse whisper again.

'*We*,' Petersen continued proudly, 'set up this whole business with Lanaghan. I got myself a job at Charlesworth's…'

Ben glanced briefly at Charlesworth and was shocked to see that he looked suddenly old, care-worn and degraded. So, Ben thought, poor old Charlesworth had been ensnared into the net and was being 'used' by this unscrupulous pair in just the same way as himself.

'…and Chloe travelled abroad setting up the contacts and supplies. Then we realized we needed a go-between – someone on the sales side. We picked you out first, but then decided your brother was better material, so

Chloe switched her – er – attentions to him.'

Ben turned his shocked, stunned gaze upon Chloe. 'But you *married* him!'

Chloe's eyes glittered. 'Is that what you think?'

'What do you mean,' Ben stammered, 'I don't understand.'

'Really, sweetie, you're even more naïve than I had thought – and *that's* saying something. Do you remember when Jason and I were married?'

'Yes – of course. He went away one weekend – to London, and you came back together – married.' Ben replied, remembering the acute pain which the event had caused him at the time.

Slowly, Chloe shook her head. 'My dear brother fixed a "mock" ceremony. Jason was too besotted to enquire into the legality of the so-called "Registry Office." We were not legally married at all.'

'But Jason – did he know?'

'Heavens no!' Chloe cast her eyes upwards in mock horror. 'In some ways, Jason could be as narrow-minded as you.'

So, Ben thought, Chloe had never loved Jason either. In fact, he doubted whether it was in her greedy nature to love anyone beyond herself. Now, Ben could find it in his heart to pity Jason. He had been led by Chloe into a life of crime, duped by her pretence of marriage to him, and now, he, Ben, was following exactly the same path as had his twin brother.

Ben looked at her and suddenly knew he no longer cared a jot for her. The woman sitting opposite had no resemblance to the Chloe he had thought he loved. A beautiful face – yes – but masking a ruthlessly ambitious, vicious character. Ben felt numb as if all feeling were suddenly suspended.

'Now listen, Winwood,' Petersen said, whilst Chloe looked on smiling and Charlesworth sat, a hunched, broken figure in a mutilated Pompadour armchair. 'Your brother started in just the same way as you are doing. He started getting cold feet and talking wildly about getting out. *There's no way out.* You're in and we've got you! Your brother escaped us, he...'

'You mean you killed him?' Ben said.

'No. That was an accident. Nothing to do with us.'

'I don't believe you. I think you had something to do with it. I think...'

Petersen moved with the swiftness of a cheetah. He raised his hand and struck Ben a vicious blow on the side of his face – the right side. Ben fell to the ground with a dull thud, unable to save himself because his hands were still tied behind his back.

His original captor now aimed a kick at his back. 'Get up!' he snarled. Ben rolled over and as he did so he saw now who this man was. It was the sour-faced butler.

Ben scrambled to his knees, scuffing the sleeve of his jacket and the knees of his trousers because his hands were still tied behind his back. He felt the side of his face begin to swell from the blow.

'That,' said Petersen, his eyes gleaming, his mouth a hard, cruel line. 'Is just for starters.'

Charlesworth's tone, in contrast, became placating, almost sympathetic. 'We don't want any trouble, Winwood. Be a sensible chap. You're in it with us. If you try to get out, we'll have to protect ourselves. That's all there is to it.'

All, thought Ben. It was everything.

Ben felt an irrational desire to laugh. The whole thing was just like a gangster movie – and a bad one at that! He had always thought that this sort of thing only happened in fiction. Even crimes one read of in the newspapers always seemed to have an unreal quality.

'You think we're joking,' Petersen hissed, his face close to Ben's. Ben realized that this wry amusement at the ridiculous situation in which he found himself must have shown on his face.

'It's no *game*.' On the last word, Petersen hit him again on the side of the face. Ben staggered and fell again, once more scrambling to his feet scuffing his clothes in so doing.

'It's very sad,' moaned Charlesworth, 'To find you're as stupid as your brother. We had just the same trouble with him.'

'Look,' Ben found his voice. 'I didn't come here to be insulted and knocked about. Since you've raised the subject – yes, I do want out. I want no more part in this filthy business. I never guessed you two were mixed up in it.'

'Very well organized, we are,' Charlesworth said.

'I can see that. I suppose,' Ben nodded towards the rows of chairs and settees. 'The suites come here for repair and re-filling with drugs and then back to Lanaghan's. Or are there other places up and down the country too?'

He saw Charlesworth and Petersen glance at each other and knew he had guessed correctly. Lanaghan's was evidently one of many shops receiving Pompadour suites in cerise – he just happened to be in Ben's area.

Finding confidence because he was seeing things so clearly, Ben continued. 'Where do you keep the stuff?' Then as the thought occurred to him. 'Out there in that bunker?'

Charlesworth half-rose to his feet, and Petersen started forward.

Ben nodded with satisfaction. 'Oh yes, I remember our friend here digging in it. He *was* looking for treasure, of a sorts, wasn't he? Quite a good little cover. Private golf course, disused club house, miles from anywhere. Near the sea, too. Come by sea, does it? Little boats creeping over the water at night, just like the smugglers of old. Oh yes – very neat. I've got to hand it to you!'

'He knows too much,' muttered Petersen, turning towards Charlesworth, who sank back into his chair and grunted.

'Look, Winwood. We don't want any bloodshed but...'

'I suppose my brother's death was enough, eh?'

It all fell into place with blinding clarity. This was what had happened to Jason. Uncannily, Ben was treading the very same path as his twin brother. This, and probably everything which had led up to it over the last twelve months, had all happened before – to Jason.

And Jason was dead – killed in a car crash after a visit, which Ben now realized had been to Charlesworth's estate, with a mysterious bruise on his right cheek, his trousers and jacked scuffed and his wrists marked in some way.

The very same marks which Ben now bore as a result of the rough treatment of the last hour or so.

'I told you we had nothing to do with Jason's death. It was an accident. Petersen and him,' Charlesworth nodded towards his 'butler', 'saw it happen.'

This was a surprise to Ben. 'How?'

'They were foll … travelling behind your brother and saw the car run off the road.'

'They didn't come forward at the inquest.'

Petersen laughed. 'You don't really expect we would have done, do you?'

'No.'

'Now,' Charlesworth said. 'Want your solemn oath that you'll think no more of this nonsense of quitting. Don't want to harm you or – or anyone belonging to you,' Ben felt a stab of fear at his words, 'but we will if you endanger us.'

'Come on,' Petersen's face was close to his, his eyes glittering, his hand raised again.

Ben glanced at it, but his fear suddenly fell away from him. He felt an enormous calm settle on him. He tried to think of some non-committal reply. 'I don't seem to have any choice,' he murmured. He waited for their reaction, but surprisingly they accepted his remark as acquiescence, and immediately Ben felt the tension slacken.

'Untie his wrists,' Charlesworth said. 'Beats me why we have to act like something out of a gangster movie. Uncivilized, I call it.'

There, thought Ben with wry amusement, spoke a true-blue aristocrat. How, he wondered, had a man like Charlesworth with his background and wealth become involved in such shady dealings? Ben glanced at Petersen. He wondered if he were the main man behind all this and had involved Charlesworth by some devious method. Now he came to study Petersen in his new role, Ben could see he was cold, calculating and utterly ruthless. No doubt he had involved Charlesworth by blackmail, or something similar.

'Right,' Petersen said as he cut the cord

tying Ben's wrists. 'You're free to go. You'll find your car parked in the lane at the back of this club-house, about five hundred yards away, with all your gear in it.'

Ben turned towards the door. He couldn't get out fast enough.

'Remember,' Petersen called after him. 'There's no escape – so watch it!'

Ben banged the door behind him and walked swiftly round the tumble-down building. He began to run across the ground between the golf course and the lane, beyond caring whether the men in the hut saw him and were amused.

He was breathless by the time he reached the lane, but thankful to see his car parked innocently a short distance away.

He dragged open the door and fell into the driving seat. The keys were in the ignition. He turned them and the engine sprang into life. He engaged gear, released the hand-brake and let in the clutch with a jerk, the car leaping forward. The engine stalled and he had to repeat the operation. This time his move away was smoother In his haste to escape, Ben never gave a thought to fastening his safety belt. He reached over and from the glove compartment extracted a packet of cigarettes and a lighter he always kept there.

With fingers which still trembled, and awkwardly with one hand, he managed to light a cigarette. He glanced in the driving mirror, anxiously, but the lane behind him was clear. He joined the main road and turned for home. His foot hard down on the accelerator the car shot forward. He glanced at the car clock. It was a little after six-thirty in the morning. As he swiftly put some distance between himself and Charlesworth's estate he began to feel a little safer.

Safe! God, that was ironic! *He would never be safe again.* Nor would his family. At the thought of the round, laughing faces of his four children – and Jean – he felt suddenly cold. Funny, but he had never thought of Chloe as his 'family'.

He had gone a good twenty miles before he became aware of a black car behind him. At first he thought nothing of it. There was quite a bit of traffic on the road now, and there was nothing remarkable about the car behind him. But as the miles passed and the traffic thinned, cars passed each other or were passed, or turned off in different directions, the pattern changed.

But the black car remained tucked in behind Ben.

He began to take more notice of it and to

try and see the occupants in his driving mirror. But the car was keeping a safe distance between them and the image in his mirror was indistinct. All he could see was that there were two people in the following car – he believed them to be men, but could not be absolutely sure at this distance.

On and on the two cars went. Normally Ben would have stopped for a rest and perhaps a meal on such a long journey, but the menacing car behind made him put his foot down harder and keep going. One hundred miles, two hundred miles. The black car was still there. It was still there twenty miles from Melchester, and by this time Ben found the fear prickling the back of his neck. Beads of sweat stood out on his forehead. He knew now they were following him. He felt the web tightening about him yet again. There was no way out, there never could be. He had been trapped by his own folly, and now he had to serve a life sentence – of criminal activity.

The road ahead was straight and clear. The rolling moors of Yorkshire fell away on either side. A solitary tree flashed occasionally by the windows. Suddenly, Ben knew this must have been exactly how Jason had felt on the day he had died. Ben had, during the past year, followed the same path as his twin brother. He saw it all so clearly now. Maybe because they had been twins they had not been so *un*alike as Ben had always thought. What was it his mother had said soon after Jason's death? Ben tried to remember her words.

'That's the only real difference there ever was between you, Ben, if only you could see it. You were never *quite* so pushing as Jason. Not quite so ruthless. You always seemed to develop a conscience if anything seemed to get a little out of hand.'

Ben sighed. Well, things had certainly got out of hand. A year ago with Jason, and now here he was in the same position. Trapped!

Jason's way out had been death and Ben knew, with certainly, that Jason had deliberately crashed his car to commit suicide as being the only way he could extricate himself. It would never have entered his head that he ought to stay alive and try to put things right. He wouldn't have spared a second's thought for all the victims of the drug-pushing racket he'd been helping to run for several years. He just wanted to get himself out of trouble and as life had lost all quality, death had been the only answer – for Jason.

But what was the answer for Ben?

He felt his mind begin to float in a very strange manner. He was aware of the road ahead, of his hands on the driving wheel, gripping it with a tense fierceness. It would be so easy. He knew what he had to do to end it all, to escape from the clutches of these rogues. Just as Jason had done. There was a slight curve in the road and on the bend a tree. All he had to do was just to let the car go straight ahead.

The wheels ate up the road. The tree came nearer and nearer and nearer...

Chapter Eleven

The blast of a police siren made Ben jump, rousing from his deep thought. He saw immediately that the car was halfway over into the wrong lane and heading off the road, directly for a tree! Ben wrenched at the steering wheel and the car, swerving suddenly, regained its correct position on the road.

The police car passed him and signalled him to slow down. There was a layby some distance up the road and the police patrol car drew into this and stopped. Ben drew into the layby and stopped behind the police car. He remained in the driving seat. The driver of the patrol car got out and began to walk towards Ben. At that moment Ben noticed the black car, which had been following him all the way from Norfolk, cruise slowly past. He glanced up and for a brief moment met the furious eyes of Petersen in the passenger seat of the black car.

Ben's intuition had been correct. Petersen had been following him.

The constable tapped on the window and Ben wound it down.

'Now, sir.' The constable leant his elbow on the car window frame and bent his head to look in at Ben. His face showed concern, but to Ben's surprise, neither antagonism nor censure.

'May I see your driving licence and certificate of insurance, please?'

'Oh – er...' Ben felt in his pocket and pulled out his wallet. His fingers trembled slightly as he extracted the requisite documents and handed them to the constable. There was a pause whilst the officer straightened up and examined the licence and insurance certificate. He bent again and handed them back to Ben.

'Winwood, I see your name is, sir. *Benjamin* Winwood.'

'Yes, that's right.'

'You seemed to be driving somewhat unsteadily, Mr Winwood. We've been following for about half-a-mile. Just before that bend in the road back there, you appeared to swerve once or twice and then looked as if you might run off the road into that tree. Would have been a nasty accident, that, sir.'

'Yes, yes, it would.'

'Have you been drinking at all?'

'What – no, no I haven't.'

'I shall have to ask you to take the breath test. Are you willing to co-operate?'

'Yes, yes, of course.'

The constable returned to his patrol car, spoke briefly to his companion, and then returned to Ben.

Numbly Ben followed the instructions the officer gave him, blowing into the bag for approximately fourteen seconds. He noticed, as he handed the bag back to the constable, that the yellow crystals in the bag had discoloured slightly. He had never been asked to take one of these tests before and knew nothing about the procedure, and so was obliged to wait until the officer had examined the bag.

'Well, sir,' the constable's head appeared at the car window again. 'That seems to be negative.'

'Well, I haven't been drinking. Not this early in the day anyway. And I don't drink much, at any time.'

'I see, sir. Do you feel unwell at all?'

'I – er, I don't really know. I'm sorry, it sounds feeble, but I – I can't seem to recall what happened. Perhaps I had some sort of blackout and yet, I was vaguely aware...' He hesitated. He couldn't very well admit that he had been so busy thinking about the mess he was in that he had lost his concentration.

Another minute and he too, like Jason, would have ended up a lifeless body in a mangled wreck of a car. Ben began to shake from head to foot as he realized how close to death he had been. But he knew too, that it had not been his intention to crash as a means of escape, only that reliving his brother's life so closely had brought him to the brink of destruction. He did not want to die. He had to live. There were Jean and the children.

Somehow he must find a way...

Ben passed a hand wearily across his forehead. His hair flopped forward into his eyes. Irrationally he remembered that he had meant to get a haircut earlier in the week and had not had the time.

The police constable was watching him. 'I see you have a nasty bruise on the side of your face, sir. How did that happen?'

Ben fingered his cheek gingerly. 'That? Oh – er – I tried to argue with a door, yes – a swing door.' He attempted to laugh. 'Silly things, aren't they, if you don't watch it?'

'Mmm,' was the only reply.

There was a pause, then the constable murmured, more to himself than to Ben. 'And your name's *Winwood.* Mmm. Wait here a moment, sir, will you?'

Ben watched as the constable went back to the patrol car. He opened the driver's door and sat down on the seat, half-in, half-out of the car, talking to his colleague. For some minutes they appeared deep in conversation, then the constable returned to Ben.

'I'd like you to come to the station with us, Mr Winwood. I think it wise you don't try to drive any further just now, don't you?'

'But I must get home,' Ben protested.

At that moment, out the corner of his eye, Ben saw the black car slide past again, in the opposite direction, waiting, watching, like a huge black vulture.

'I must get away, I must get home,' Ben repeated, his voice a little hysterical.

'Where is "home"?'

'Melchester.'

'Over twenty miles yet. A long way, Mr Winwood, if you're feeling badly. You come along with us to the station, and we'll see.'

'Are you going to charge me?'

'Well, sir, you may be liable for prosecution for driving without due care and attention. But come along with us now. We'll have your car collected by a garage of your choice and see about you getting home.'

'I did want to get home,' Ben said again, but this time without conviction. At least if he went with the policemen, he would be safe from the black car.

Ben locked his car and followed the policeman. Automatically, he straightened his crooked tie and flicked the hair back from falling across his forehead.

As the police car sped smoothly towards the police station, Ben sat in the back seat and closed his eyes, trying to calm his troubled emotions. With half an ear he heard the two officers talking in the front seat. They were no longer talking to him or even about him. They were chatting as might any two workmates. Then suddenly, their conversation made Ben sit bolt upright.

'What's the time, Mike.'

The constable in the passenger's seat glanced at his watch.

'Just gone two-forty-five.'

'Ah – I wonder what won the two thirty. My Dad just about put his shirt on a horse in that. I told him not to be so daft, but you know him.' His colleague laughed.

'Tut-tut, your Dad and the gee-gees!'

But Ben was not listening. It was the words 'two-thirty' which had struck a chord in his befuddled memory.

Two-thirty! And it was two-forty-five now. Then his accident must have occurred just after two-thirty.

The same time exactly that Jason had been killed one year ago today!

At the station he was handed over to the station sergeant, who was as courteous as the constable had been, and even kindly. It was not the sort of treatment Ben had expected to receive. From his youth the echoes of his fear of the burly station sergeant as he handed in his find, still haunted him. The truth now was indeed a different story. It was the same station and even the same Sergeant Porter who had been so kind to him when he had come here to identify Jason.

'You may smoke if you wish, Mr Winwood,' the sergeant pushed an ashtray across the table.

'Thanks.' Ben fumbled in his pocket for his cigarettes and lit one. He inhaled deeply, and then coughed.

It tasted foul!

He coughed again and ground out the cigarette in the ashtray. He saw the sergeant watching him curiously. Ben cleared his throat nervously. 'I'm really sorry about the trouble I've caused. I – honestly don't know what happened. As I told your constable, it

219

must have been some sort of blackout – or – or something,' Ben finished lamely.

The sergeant nodded sympathetically. 'It can happen to the best of us, Mr Winwood. But you would be well advised not to drive for some time. And might I suggest you see a doctor?'

Ben looked up in surprise.

'Just for a check up, Mr Winwood.'

'Yes, yes. Perhaps you're right. I'll see my own when I get home.'

'Do you feel all right now? I could arrange for a doctor to see you here if…'

'No, no, please. I'm all right now.'

'About you getting home…'

'Look, if it's all the same to you, I'll put up at an hotel – if there is one somewhere near – for the night and – if you agree, drive home tomorrow.'

The sergeant thought for a moment. 'I'd be happier if you took a taxi home. Just until you've seen a doctor. That bruise,' the sergeant gestured towards Ben's face. 'The constable tells me you banged into a door.'

Ben nodded.

'Perhaps that's had more effect than you think. I should get it looked at if I were you. If you see a doctor today and he says you're okay to drive, then I see no reason why you shouldn't drive tomorrow if you feel all right.'

Ben nodded agreement.

'Good. I'll ring for a taxi to take you to a pub not far away. They put up the odd commercial traveller. They'll find you a room all right. Then I'll ask a local doctor to call on you.'

Ben looked up at the sergeant who stood up. 'You're – very kind. Thank you.'

Sergeant Porter looked down at Ben with sudden compassion as if guessing that more lay behind the near-accident than Ben was admitting.

'We're not here just to run folks in, you know, Mr Winwood. We like to *help* people in any way we can. In *any* way.'

Dumbly Ben nodded. 'Yes,' he said and his voice was a whisper. How he would have liked to have confided in the kindly sergeant, to have poured out the whole sorry tale, but something held it back. He must have time to think first, to decide just what he ought to do.

The doctor, who arrived about two hours later at the public house to visit Ben, was middle-aged, bright and breezy.

'Nasty bruise there, but you're quite fit.

Good for another forty years or more. I'll ring the sergeant and let him know.'

'I can drive home tomorrow then?'

'In my opinion, yes. But take it steady and at the first sign of any trouble – stop.'

'Yes. Thanks.'

'Righto – righto. Cheerio.'

And he was gone as quickly as he had come.

Ben lay back on the narrow bed and fell fast asleep.

Sergeant Porter said to the police constable on duty at the station desk. 'There'll be a bloke called Winwood come for these car keys and his licence this morning. Now, we'll be wanting to question him again. At least I understand Superintendent Spencer will.'

'Right you are, sir,' murmured the constable at the desk continuing to write without looking up.

'Will you get Detective Superintendent Spencer for me, and put the call through to my office.'

'Yes, sir.'

A few moments later, Sergeant Porter, swinging slightly from side to side in his swivel chair, was talking to Superintendent Spencer of the C.I.D.

'I thought you'd be interested to know there had been a further development in the "Winwood Saga".' The sergeant went on to give full details of the near-accident involving Ben Winwood.

'Following your instructions last week, sir, my patrolmen had orders to watch out for his car number and report on any unusual movements.'

'And?'

'You received my report last Wednesday that he'd been seen heading south out of our area?'

'Yup. I got on to that straightaway and got co-operation from other counties. I know where he's been. I'll tell you in a minute. You tell me first what you know – anymore than just the fact of a possible charge for dangerous driving?'

'Well, I've been making a few enquiries of my own. Mottershead, who brought Benjamin Winwood in yesterday, pointed out the distinct similarity between the near-accident yesterday and one some time ago. I looked it up. It was exactly – believe it or believe it not – a year ago yesterday, at least by the day, Friday the thirteenth it was last year, that his brother Jason Winwood was killed on the same spot, in much the same way as he would have been yesterday if Mottershead hadn't blasted his siren at him. *And* the accident would have occurred at about the same time of day too. Uncanny, isn't it?'

'Mmm,' Superintendent Spencer replied. 'Interesting. You know we came to a full stop in our enquiries after his brother was killed last year. But as I told you at the time we've kept an eye on Jason's former associates – and on Benjamin Winwood too. Things have started to move again recently and we're hopeful of getting some sort of positive lead very soon.'

'That girl who died – outside Lanaghan's shop? Any lead there?' Porter asked.

'We're pretty sure Lanaghan has something to do with it. We had a look round his shop at that time, but without anything definite it's pretty difficult to move.'

'Too true! And the other "associates"?'

'Ah, now here it gets *very* interesting. You know Benjamin Winwood's changed a lot since his brother's death. Even took over his brother's job and – by all accounts – the widow as well?'

'Yes,' replied Porter. 'When he came into the station yesterday, I could see how much he had altered since he came to identify his brother. Ordinarily, I might not have recalled his previous appearance so clearly, but because of your continued interest in him, I kept a mental picture of him as I remembered him from then. His whole appearance has altered. He's snappily dressed now, and smarter, but he seemed nervous yesterday, not himself at all. Looked – lost, somehow. I must admit I felt a bit sorry for the bloke.'

Spencer sniffed somewhat contemptuously. 'If he's been involved with this drug business – as I suspect – I should save your sympathy.'

'Well, I suppose you have a point, sir. You were saying you knew where he'd been before the near-accident occurred?'

'Yes. He went to spend a golfing weekend at the country estate of Lewis Charlesworth – Chairman of the Board of Directors of Charlesworths.'

Sergeant Porter gave a low whistle.

'Of course, we don't know what went on in the privacy of Charlesworth's mansion,' Spencer continued, 'but I do know that Winwood left yesterday morning – very early – in a helluva hurry *and* was followed all the way from Norfolk by a big, black car, carrying Petersen, Charlesworth's Managing Director. What they didn't know that for the whole of the journey, various police cars – your patrolmen included – have kept their movements under observation.'

'Do you think Charlesworth and Petersen are involved?'

Spencer said, 'This is the area we need a positive lead on before we can really take action. I can get nothing on them. Now, if we raid Lanaghan's shop, find something and run him in, perhaps even getting Winwood in the process, I'm *still* not getting at the Big Boys – the organizers. *They're* the ones I *really* want.'

'Quite. You know – I had the feeling yesterday that Winwood almost wanted to tell me something. If ever I saw a chap who looked as if he were being driven along the road to Hell by the Devil himself, it was Benjamin Winwood. I'll tell you something else, too. He has a nasty bruise on the right side of his face, done, he says, by a swing door. But on looking up the records on Jason Winwood, there was a note of a similar bruise on his face, which, the pathologist said had been caused before the accident.'

'Interesting. Could be they weren't toeing the line and the Big Boys roughed them up a bit. Let's hope Benjamin comes to his senses and comes back to see us, before he ends up like his brother,' Spencer said drily, 'But I doubt he will. Right then, Porter. Thanks. Keep in touch. Cheers.'

At about twelve o'clock Ben approached the desk a little hesitantly. 'Er – excuse me.'

The constable raised his head. 'Yes, sir. What can I do for you?'

Ben cleared his throat nervously and flicked back his hair which was falling into his eyes. 'I've – er – called to collect my car keys and licence.'

'Ah yes, sir.' The police officer reached to his right and picked up the licence and keys. 'You're Mr Winwood?'

'Yes.'

'Going straight home now, are you?'

'Yes – yes.'

'This address in your licence – is it correct? Twenty-two Montpelier Crescent, Melchester?'

Ben hesitated. He had completely forgotten to have the address on his licence changed when he had left Jean and moved in with Chloe.

'Is that your present address, sir?' the constable said again.

'Er – yes. Yes, it is.'

As he left the station, Ben realized that

that was exactly where he was heading.

Home – to Jean.

If only she would have him!

As he gained the main road, he reached across into the glove compartment for cigarettes and lighter.

He lit one and drew.

It tasted as awful as the one he'd smoked whilst talking to Sergeant Porter the previous day, soon after the near-accident.

Ben threw the cigarette out of the window. Then, after a moment's thought, the whole cigarette packet went the same way.

Chapter Twelve

Ben drew up outside his house – the one where he'd lived most of his married life with his wife and children.

Suddenly he couldn't wait to see her – and the children. Couldn't wait to feel those chubby hands grasping his knees and bright, beaming faces upturned in greeting.

He felt unusually nervous, shy almost, as if he had come a-courting. As, indeed, he had in a way.

He rang the doorbell and waited. Then he rang again. The house was silent. No one came to the door. There was no sound of children's voices. Ben felt a sudden stab of fear. Surely Petersen and Charlesworth hadn't carried out their threats already.

He hammered on the door in panic. Still no answer. He peered through the lounge window. It was just the same as he remembered it. Comfortingly, reassuringly the same. Toys scattered everywhere, newspapers and magazines strewn haphazardly on the furniture. Even the hard, uncomfortable settee suddenly dear and familiar. It all looked so ordinary, so uncomplicated – and somehow, so safe!

But the house was silent. Ben's heart hammered painfully and his hands were suddenly clammy. Then he remembered. It was Saturday, and afternoon now. Jean would have taken the children to the park. He ran round the house and down the path to the car, his footsteps light with relief.

Ben stood for a moment watching Jean before she saw him. She was sitting on a park bench watching the children on the swings, her hands pushed deep into the pockets of her old raincoat, beneath which the hem of her summer dress showed. On her feet were flat-heeled, serviceable shoes. Her unruly hair was blowing in the slight breeze, but she was smiling gently to herself, as she watched her children – their children – with fond eyes. Overwhelmingly, Ben longed to take her in his arms and hold her close. Dear, untidy, lovable Jean!

'Jean!' Ben's voice was a hesitant, hoarse whisper.

She started forward and half rose from the bench before she realized who it was.

'Ben!'

He watched the expression on her face

change. At first there was surprise, then, as she noted his appearance – the stooping, rounded shoulders, the dishevelled suit, the tie a little crooked, the lock of hair falling over his forehead, a smile quirked the corner of her mouth. Tentatively, as if afraid to hope, afraid to believe, she said again. 'Why – Ben!'

Did he imagine it or did she really emphasize the name – Ben?

He sat down beside her and leant forward, his elbows on his knees, his hands clasped. 'Jean – I don't know where to begin...'

At that moment there was a shriek from the direction of the swings and they both looked up to see their four children racing across the grass towards them. At least three raced and one – Gabrielle – toddled. But all four had wide, welcoming grins on their faces. They hurled themselves at him as if in one excited, clamorous bundle.

'Daddy!'

'Have you come to play with us?'

'Come and sail my boat.'

'Come home with us to tea. He may, mayn't he, Mummy? Oh, do come!'

'Wait for me,' a plaintive wail seemed to demand and Ben scooped Gabrielle into his arms. The child fastened her chubby arms tightly about his neck. Ben closed his eyes. *This* was what he had missed. After the hell of his nightmarish existence of the past few weeks and months, to be once more encircled by his little girl's arms, felt like Heaven indeed!

He held her fiercely, protectively, only now realizing how very much he had had and had thrown away. Was it too late? Could he come back to this loving, happy, carefree circle.

He looked at Jean and saw she was smiling happily.

'Run along, now, children, for a while longer,' she said.

'Aw, Mum,' the protests were unanimous, but surprisingly they obeyed. Perhaps their child's instinct told them that this meeting between their parents after so long was important – for all of them.

'Now, Ben. What is it you want to tell me?'

Haltingly, he began to explain the events following Jason's death. He told Jean everything as it had happened to him – omitting nothing – like a sinner in the confessional. Jean listened silently and patiently. As he talked the words flowed more easily. Then, as he finished his tale with the events of the preceding day, he lapsed into silence.

Jean said nothing for a long time, then softly she asked. 'And now?'

Ben sighed. 'I must give myself up to the police. It's the only thing I can do. But I'll probably be in trouble, maybe even prison.'

'You'll be giving information about all the other people involved in this?'

Ben nodded.

'Will you tell them about Chloe's part in it?'

'Yes. But Jean – believe me, I haven't come back to you just because I've found that out. It was dead – or at least dying – long before yesterday.' It was the truth, but he waited anxiously for Jean to speak. He heard her give a long sigh of relief.

'I believe you,' she said softly.

Ben gripped her hand thankfully. 'I can't understand how I could have been so blind, so – so infatuated with her. She's shallow and ruthless – I see that now.'

'I think,' said Jean quietly, 'that at first you saw her as you *wanted* to see her, as you liked to remember her from when you first met – before she married Jason, or at least as we *thought* she married him. You idolized her, but that wasn't a true picture, but then as time went on and – and you seemed to – oh I don't know – you seemed to *become*

Jason, perhaps you were seeing her through his eyes and after all, he – well – he was a bit like her, wasn't he?'

'Cold and ruthless, you mean?' Ben said. 'Yes, very much so.' It was a bald statement of the truth. 'And I was weak and foolish to be taken in by it all.'

Jean reached out and took his hand. 'We all have our faults. God knows, I have mine. I know that. You shouldn't be condemned for the rest of your life for a very human weakness, at least as far as Chloe is concerned. As for the other business, well, it's not for me to have to judge you, thank goodness.'

'Jean – before I – go to the police, what I want to know is, I know I've treated you badly – terribly, but do you think you could ever forgive me? Do you understand that what happened, I seemed powerless against it?'

'Yes, Ben. I do understand. I really don't know what did happen to you, but I can see now that you've come back to me as Ben – the old Ben. The man I loved and still do. I said – when you left, do you remember, that if you ever came back as Ben – then it would be all right. And it is. I'll stand by you whatever happens.'

'Oh Jean!' Ben's voice cracked and he

gripped her hand tightly again, almost afraid to believe his good luck.

They sat there, holding hands, for some time watching their children playing on the swings, hearing their shrieks of carefree laughter.

At last Ben sighed heavily. 'I suppose I'd better get it over with.'

Jean nodded. 'I'll take the kids home.'

'I don't know how long I'll be. They might even keep me. You know – arrest me.'

'We'll be waiting, Ben, however long it is.'

Ben kissed her full on the mouth, oblivious to passers-by. He stood up and walked away quickly, before the children saw him go. Right now he couldn't face having to say 'goodbye' to them, not so soon after having been reunited with them.

It seemed an age since he had left the Byron Road Police Station, and yet it could only have been a matter of hours, for, as he walked in, he saw it was the same constable still on duty at the desk.

Ben cleared his throat. The constable looked up.

'Why, Mr Winwood. Anything wrong? Forget something, did you?'

'Er – you could say that – yes. Um – is Sergeant Porter available by any chance?'

'I think so, sir. I'll just check for you. Do sit down a moment.' The constable lifted a telephone receiver, clicked a few switches on a small switchboard and said, 'Ah, Sergeant Porter. Mr Winwood is here again and would like to see you. Yes – yes – right away, sir.' The constable replaced the receiver. 'This way, Mr Winwood, please.'

Ben found himself ushered into a small interview room furnished only with a table and two chairs, one either side of the table facing each other. Scarcely had Ben sat down in one, than the door opened and Sergeant Porter came in.

'Ah, Mr Winwood,' he smiled down at Ben and there was a wealth of satisfaction in his smile. Briskly, the police officer sat down opposite Ben, placed a sheaf of blank paper and a pen in front of him, and then his fingers clasped upon the desk, said, 'How can I help you, Mr Winwood?'

'I really don't know how to begin to tell you all this – it all seems like some terrible nightmare, so – so unbelievable.'

'Would it help you, Mr Winwood, if I were to tell you that we do know a little, I think, about what you now want to talk to me about. Since you left here earlier I've been talking to one of my colleagues who has, for the last eighteen months, probably longer, been investigating the existence of a drug-pushing organization...'

'Then you know...?'

'Not nearly enough, Mr Winwood. And this is where you can help us, isn't it?'

Ben nodded. Momentarily, the sergeant leaned towards Ben. 'And believe me, Mr Winwood, you'll not only be helping us, but yourself as well. To turn Queen's Evidence now, will certainly encourage the Court to act leniently towards you. Though, please understand I can't promise you anything. Now,' Porter added, 'where shall we begin?'

All at once Ben felt as if the tremendous weight of the fear and misery of the last few weeks and months had been lifted from him. He looked across at the open, honest, kindly face of the officer. For a fleeting moment, Ben saw again Petersen's cold, ruthless face, the man whom Ben now believed was the ring-leader. He'd dance at Petersen's funeral all right, maybe not literally, but he, Ben, would see Petersen brought to justice.

Ben began to speak, the words tumbling out in relief, like the opening of flood gates.

Swiftly, Sergeant Porter began to write.

The publishers hope that this book has given you enjoyable reading. Large Print Books are especially designed to be as easy to see and hold as possible. If you wish a complete list of our books please ask at your local library or write directly to:

Dales Large Print Books
Magna House, Long Preston,
Skipton, North Yorkshire.
BD23 4ND